I0593578

THE
LOST TABLETS
OF
IYAR

J.H. Ellis

This is a work of fiction. Names, characters, places, brands, media, and incidents are either the product of the author's imagination or are used fictitiously.

Copyright © 2022 by Judith Howard Ellis

Cover design by Amanda Kelsey of Razzle Dazzle Design
Book interior and e-book design by Amit Dey

All rights reserved. Without limiting the rights under copyright reserved above, no part of this publication may be reproduced, stored in or introduced into a retrieval system, or transmitted, in any form, or by any means (electronic, mechanical, photocopying, recording, or otherwise) without the prior written permission of the above copyright owner of this book.

ISBN-13: 978-0-9831548-3-9

In loving memory of Poppy

For every time you nudged me with the words:
"What about the book, Baby?"

The secret things belong unto the Lord our God: but those things which are revealed belong unto us and to our children forever, that we may do all the words of this law.

Deuteronomy 29:29
(King James Version)

CHAPTER ONE

THE DESERT HORSEMEN

The phantoms moaned to Iyar on the desert wind. To quiet them, he reached for a cup nestled near his matted pillow. Empty. Was it midday or yesterday morning when he finished the Midvar wine? He scattered his blankets, searching for a wine jar, until his thick fingers landed on an Edrei cushion embellished with emeralds and rubies. He clung to it, then let it go.

Iyar stumbled to stand in the large tent, digging his toes into a thick rug patterned with rings and stars, another luxury from Edrei discovered in a shop dusted by spider webs. Iyar had ordered the rug carried to his caravan outside Edrei's city gates in skin-frying heat.

Such finds had earned Iyar the reputation of importing the most desirable novelties, and he filled his tent with treasures he kept for himself. For a moment, he wished he had amassed fewer textiles, platters, and baskets as he squirreled through the tent. Where did Naphtali store the wine? Ah. Near a pile of wool, clay jars stood like soldiers awaiting orders.

A Midvar vinedresser had haggled with him over the wine for hours, and Iyar squabbled about every shekel. The bargaining game with the vinedresser forced Iyar to stay another night in Midvar's capital city with an unexpected result; he'd met a dark-haired lyre player.

The woman, Raushanna, heard Iyar hum along with her melodies in a dingy tavern and invited him to sing with her. Within a moment, he was beside her, ignoring the jeers of his friends, who stood stunned when he delivered a tender falsetto.

Iyar sang with his eyes shut; his hands looped over his pot-round belly:

> *Love captured me at dawn,*
> *Filled me with joy at noon,*
> *Carried me away at sunset.*
> *Protected me beneath the midnight stars.*
> *May I know your affection always,*
> *Because your love crosses seven hills,*
> *Never forgetting,*
> *An olive tree blooms forever for love for me.*

Iyar, concealing tears as he finished, bowed his head. His mother sang those words every day to his father, Yissack, including the day she found him lifeless on the street in the City of Kings. Iyar and his siblings clung to the song even after their mother joined their family ancestors. Iyar sang the song as a lullaby, each time bemused, because his three children, when only babes, pestered him to carry them to the seven hills.

After Iyar guided the song's last words into a hush, Raushanna lifted her lyre toward him. She stood a short distance from him, tall and shapely as a warrior-goddess summoning him to the battle of songs.

"To Lord Iyar," she said. "A singer of merit for the generations and eons."

One of Iyar's merchant friends, a grumpy man who never expressed happiness about anything except for beer, overturned his table with a boisterous jerk. "Iyar has a voice. By the cockroaches crawling in the storehouses, I wouldn't have believed it if he hadn't chirped like a lovesick bird."

Couples hugged. Craggy-faced tavern customers smiled in pride. For a few honeyed days after that night, Iyar dedicated his thoughts to music and not money. He sent Naphtali throughout the bazaar to locate incense and textiles for their caravan while sitting for uninterrupted hours with Raushanna. The pair revived old folk hymns, some from Seth, and some from Midvar. They composed new songs.

They invited other musicians. Some declined, blinded by the accepted tradition that forbade a woman to play the lyre. Raushanna, the daughter and granddaughter of musicians, shrugged off tradition one afternoon while biting into a tomato in a patron's courtyard scented with jasmine.

"None of my ancestors abandoned their instruments. Why should I deny my inheritance?"

Later that day, a gossipy aristocrat lounged with them in the courtyard. She had assured them that Midvar's Queen Erela, once she heard about their music, intended to attend a performance. Raushanna acknowledged the compliment but hid her expression with a swing of her hair, leading Iyar to believe she found the gossip tantalizing and untrue.

Indeed, the queen never joined a tavern or courtyard where they played during Iyar's stay in Midvar, and for once,

Iyar didn't care about preening. Nothing else mattered in the presence of Raushanna, who, with a whisper, enticed him to sing and he obeyed, songs gushing from him in wild rivers he refused to dam.

Iyar unplugged a wine jar and poured a cup. He hoped Raushanna's newest suitor brought her joy even if he were part of the priestly class. Maybe the dull haze on the man's face was love. If anguished affection entrapped the priest's soul, Iyar understood. For at each tilted dune, miles away in this desert, Raushanna's music drifted through his thoughts, baptizing him in sorrow.

Foolish.

Iyar slobbered the wine, filling his mouth until the liquid seeped in a tiny trail from beard to belly. Memories of Raushanna blurred too.

Warm sunlight peered through the tent's opening, inviting him to view the setting sun. Iyar made his way to the tent entrance, where Naphtali curled in sleep, snoring enough for two people.

Iyar jabbed his heel into Naphtali's left side. The boy muttered in pain, but Iyar exhaled in relief. Kicking the slave again was tempting, but he lifted his foot from Naphtali's side and steadied himself. Two nights lay ahead before they reached the City of Kings. A bruised boy would be a burden on his caravan, so Iyar stomped from the tent, clutching the wine cup.

Framed by clouds, an orange sun burned. He never tired of watching the sun linger, then slide into the horizon. In the desert, away from the busyness of the City of Kings, sunset beckoned him. During these hours, Iyar felt most quiet. When he and siblings, Abigail and Eli, were children, they huddled at the window and hopped throughout the house like impatient sparrows eager for Father to come home.

Once Yissak arrived, he gathered his children to him with stiff fingers from hours of sewing and stacking textiles. Even now, Iyar remembered his father's tales about murderous thieves, corrupt priests, and slothful nobles. He also never forgot his father's face, a face identical to his. Round, the shade of ripe barley, centered by cool blue eyes.

In many things, Iyar wasn't his father's son. Yissack's eyes never glinted with cold delight when he witnessed cruelty. Yissack practiced patience and kindness, while Iyar couldn't name a virtue he prized. Before that thought exploded into more torment, and as his stomach soured and his hands shook, Iyar gulped more wine.

The desert wind sped up into heavy gusts, and the horses squealed in reply. The fronds of the stout palm trees that leaned like temple guardians over the camp swayed as if twisted by unseen hands.

Desert flies, buoyed forward by the winds, dashed toward Iyar's ankles. He howled when he felt the stings and dropped his cup. Midvar wine dripped into the sand like blood.

"Vermin!"

Iyar waved his muscled arms, swatting the terrorizing flies.

"Foulness! By every crawling thing in the desert, by every pig and donkey, perish!"

He stopped swatting flies when he glimpsed four riders racing from the west with the setting sun behind them.

The four sped toward the tent, uninhibited by dunes, their black steeds wearing neither insignias nor banners to identify kings and kingdoms. Sea pirates? Perhaps they tracked Iyar's carts inland from Edrei. In the taverns, merchants whispered about rowdy sailors choosing to plunder the cities and the seas, depending on the season or if their food and beer supplies were low. If true, the ruffians traveled with stealth in the desert. But as he studied them, the horsemen seemed too regal for thieves.

Iyar adjusted his stained tunic and toweled his face, as if the movements would make his vision clearer and his head pound less.

He shouted over his shoulder. "Naphtali! My sword. The men!"

Iyar waited for Naphtali to stir inside the tent. Yesterday, Iyar had rewarded the hired soldiers with rest after their journey from the east because they would reach the City of Kings soon— in time to sell garments and trinkets as the kingdom prepared for Lord Shammah's royal nuptials. Iyar had surprised himself when he offered the soldiers a wine jar and even permitted the exhausted Naphtali a sip. Had Iyar known pirates lurked in this region, he wouldn't have been so generous.

Within moments, Naphtali was outside, yelling at the soldiers in a second tent. "Your swords, slumbering jackals!"

Iyar nodded as he overheard Naphtali. The merchant counted beneath his breath: "One shekel. Two shekels. Three shekels. Four."

It was unkind. Petty. But slaves and soldiers followed Iyar's commands, especially when foes threatened their master and his property.

"Five shekels. Six," Iyar continued.

He extended his right arm. Naphtali, stumbling slightly, slapped a sword into Iyar's palm before Iyar counted to seven. Iyar nodded in coy approval. Naphtali had followed Iyar's training, and they'd practiced this tactic often. Carrying a dagger, Naphtali shuffled his lanky body in the sand beside Iyar.

"Ready," Naphtali said. Iyar knew he was fighting drowsiness.

Iyar felt regret. Giving Naphtali a sip of wine was reckless. "Awaken, boy."

"Vipers crawl and bite from a drunken man's table," Naphtali said.

"Rebellious one," Iyar said. "Expect a beating."

"I would expect nothing less."

The merchant bobbed his head left and right as the seven soldiers formed a half-circle around the merchant and," Iyar said.

Naphtali and the soldiers lifted their weapons.

With hoods shadowing their faces, the four horsemen urged their galloping horses forward, tongues of flame surging from their nostrils.

Iyar scrambled to recall whether he had encountered assailants like these. He'd battled giant Mikana and outwitted those who practiced the night arts in the desert. But he'd never seen the likes of the four riders with their steeds blowing fire.

Iyar clutched his sword and raised it, but the weapon sprang from his hand, loosened by a harsh wind gust. Spears, swords, and daggers also flew from the grips of Naphtali and the soldiers.

Iyar spat. "They must be pirates. Or renegade priests with potions and spells."

"No, not pirates, my lord." Naphtali scanned the dunes and skies. "Sand sorcerers."

The four riders halted within an arm's length of Iyar. On horseback, they stood shoulders taller than Iyar and his men, their faces obscured by garments shimmering with sunset golds. For long moments, no one spoke as the horses snorted smokeless blue-and-gold flames.

Iyar's neck and hands dripped with sweat. How many shekels could he gain for the magnificent clothing these men wore? What weaver did they use? What artisan had captured that color of dye? Thoughts of money comforted him. As his father had told Iyar many times, wise men overcame fear, and merchants couldn't afford it. Wise men slipped past sea dragons in heavy fog and evaded thieves in sandstorms. And in Iyar's mind, merchants hoarded money and, when necessary, traded with dragons and thieves. Foolish men never conquered fear and never earned respect or money.

"What do you want, desert raiders? Gold? Lapis lazuli? I am willing to sell. Or trade." Iyar felt his words sounded strong and authoritative, especially with the fire-horses breathing nearby.

One rider dismounted, and when his feet touched sand, the earth rumbled. Iyar caught his breath and Naphtali shrieked. One soldier fainted.

The man's hood slipped to his shoulders, revealing a lion-stare that could batter stone.

"We are not pirates," the man said. "We are not renegade priests or sorcerers. We care nothing for your bounty from Edrei. We do not need your Midvar wine or your precious cushion."

Iyar heaved for air as he rummaged through his mind for scraps of humility and diplomacy. The man knew details about Iyar's caravan. "Friends, is there an altar that requires my homage? Or an idol I have not made? Sacrifices I am prepared to give. I will spare no cost."

"I am Gabar. We do not require your offerings, Lord Iyar."

The merchant shuddered at hearing his name and felt as mighty as a chickpea when Gabar leaned toward him.

"We request a seat at your table," Gabar said.

Iyar blinked hard and rubbed freckled hands on his stomach. "You hear my words from afar and divine my name and places of travel. Your steeds spout fire. Yet you whisper a petition to sup with me? Wine has granted me a dream."

"We stand with you in this desert," Gabar said. "Should you touch my horse to feel its flame?"

The fire-snorting animal raised his head and trotted closer to Iyar. The merchant trembled, refusing to touch the horse, while marveling that he wasn't scorched. Then the horse bowed, its breath igniting a puddle of flames.

"If you promise peace, a meal is what I always have," Iyar said. "I can do nothing else. You confiscated our swords. Thief."

Their weapons fell from the sky, barely missing Iyar's toes.

Iyar stepped backward. "Are you not gods?"

"We are like Naphtali," Gabar said.

Naphtali reached for his weapon. "By the pigs and rats. Sand sorcerers."

"Yes, we roam the desert and tread hidden routes in sky and Earth," Gabar said. "We journey where you dream."

Gabar leaned toward Naphtali, and Iyar waited for the boy to collapse.

"Do you recognize your path, Naphtali?" Gabar said. "Are you willing to endure so that your lord can find his?"

"Endure what? Do you utter omens, sorcerer?" Naphtali jerked his head in a pose that mimicked a skinny bird with a stringy red crest. "Do you divine entrails of goats?"

"Tilt with the times and seasons, Naphtali. Your lord will also do the same."

Naphtali served Iyar and the four strangers with sparkling platters and jeweled cups. Iyar chatted at random, gaining a glance or a solemn gaze from his four guests, who ate like nobles at a private gathering—far from the open-mouthed chewing and guffaw-ridden feasts he attended in the Midvar tavern where he and Raushanna performed.

Iyar swallowed a chunk of bread with annoyance. Part of him wanted the men to hasten from his tent and return to whatever sky hovel they belonged, while part of him wanted them to explain who they were and how they gained their skills in the night arts.

He assumed they were sorcerers, as Naphtali said, because of the golden haze surrounding them, which both illuminated and warmed the tent. Iyar didn't fancy sorcerers, and assumed they huddled in caves and forests rather than deserts, but he was curious about the life they lived and whether he could gain a shekel or two from a business alliance.

And then, maybe not. The four horsemen sat cross-legged in his tent with its heavy, colorful fabrics, frankincense misting from an incense pot, unimpressed by Iyar's goods. Ants earned more attention. Gabar pushed away his platter. Only the center bone remained. "Few caravans cook with such precision. Thank you."

The compliment cheered Iyar. "My mother was the best cook in the City of Kings. But Naphtali prepared this meal. If he heeded my teaching, he would have kept the lamb in the fire longer. And if he didn't sleep so much, he could cook for the best houses."

Naphtali, with his sword lying near him, studied Gabar and his companions. "I live in the best house."

"Then cook like my pupil," Iyar said.

Gabar raised an eyebrow. "Perhaps cooking meals for men with cool hearts is not everything prepared for Naphtali to do."

Iyar chortled like someone tickled his stomach and toes as he, with some anxiety, tried to recall where he placed his sword.

"This is the life I've ordained for Naphtali," Iyar said. "He knows no more. He needs no more. Why do you only speak? Why is that? Your men eat, but they have not uttered a word. Why not chasten them for being impolite?"

The four didn't reply. Iyar kept talking to amuse himself. "They are mute, eh? Maybe you helped yourself to their tongues. Gabar, did you slice both their tongues and souls with your dagger?"

Iyar cupped his belly. "I remember a sailor I met long ago. A slave trader snatched the sailor's tongue after a gambling dispute. Curious, I bought the sailor a drink and told Naphtali to give the man a tablet and stylus. With a steady hand, the sailor scribbled words of gratitude for the amputation. The inability to speak, the man told me, liberated him from holding conversations with his wife, a well of infinite chatter."

Gabar folded his hands in silence. Iyar suspected the man judged his words trivial and rude.

Iyar pretended to cough, and it spurted from him like a cackle. "I am sorry your companions cannot speak. What loneliness you wrestle during your desert rides."

With their heads bowed, Gabar and his companions pealed in unison: "Every tribe and kingdom in the four corners of the earth hear our words."

An amber hue fell inside the tent, followed by an unearthly blast of a ram's horn that whipped the tent poles and rocked the ground.

Iyar grabbed his head. Like a man's fist, the wind pressed his skull and spine. When fresh sea mist entered the tent, Iyar and Naphtali stroked their faces in surprise. The seashore was days away from the desert. Naphtali scurried to the tent opening. Water cascaded outside the tent, pummeling through sand as if fountains in the earth had broken open.

"Halt." Iyar waved his arms at Gabar and the men, but the roaring continued.

Winds swelled until the upper tent flap sprung open to the night sky. Sand splattered the air and bit into Iyar's plump cheeks.

Naphtali wobbled to Iyar while pointing his sword at Gabar. "Heed my lord. Halt."

Iyar placed a hand on the boy to steady himself. Too much food had made him sluggish. "Keep your weapon raised, Naphtali. I must owe a debt to the gods or offended a crazed priest or seer. If they slay you first, maybe I will escape perdition."

Gabar lifted a hand. The upper tent cover slammed into place. The waters disappeared.

This time, only Gabar's voice filled the tent. "My companions do not speak because their voices summon desert storms and subdue them. We are unaccustomed to small words that mean little."

"What matters to them?" An anxious blush spread along Naphtali's throat.

"The destiny of the kingdom."

"There are many kingdoms. Ours is the kingdom of Seth where King Shammah reigns."

"You possess strength, Naphtali. In maturity, you will be stronger still."

"I'm a slave. I'm strong only for Lord Iyar."

"King Shammah would count himself highly favored if he knew you. He also would treat you with great kindness."

Gabar turned to Iyar. "You, however, have fallen out of favor with the king, have you not?"

Iyar gulped. The sorcerer-stranger knew too much. "I do not pander to kings."

"Yet you reveled in your friendship with King Aikah."

"We perceived kingdom commerce the same way."

"Bribes undo justice."

"Money resolves challenges."

"A view shared by many who hoard it," Gabar said. "As King Shammah warned, do not neglect the poor, for their champion deserves fear and glory."

"King Shammah is young, untried," Iyar said. "He does not understand the transactions of goods or the self-imposed chaos that persists with the poor. Give them food and shelter. They lack ambition to rise among the classes to gain wealth."

The merchant saw Naphtali bite his lip and squirm during his summation, but Iyar didn't care. Neither Shammah nor the impoverished understood the intricacies of commerce.

Gabar and his companions rose. They spoke in a formidable mutter. "A reckoning is coming. Not long from now, a choice will come to you, Iyar. Drink from the cup that delights the strong on Earth. Or drink from the cup of sacrifice. The true tabernacle is the only refuge."

The four fell silent and sat. Iyar didn't know how to respond. Cups and tabernacles. He rubbed his midsection. The lamb fat wasn't settling well. Greasy meat and omens promised nightmares, and Iyar already struggled with phantoms.

"Lord Iyar," Gabar said, "we must impose upon you once more. Can you and Naphtali spare room in your tent?"

Iyar didn't know how he could deny him, even though it was impolite for Gabar to mention how King Shammah chided Iyar for lending to the poor at high rates. But Iyar couldn't demand an apology. Swords and spears from Iyar and his men couldn't slay a roaring whirlwind, fiery horses, and sea mist.

Most of all, despite his stately height and intense stare, gentleness emanated from Gabar like night winds brushing the Earth, a contradiction unnerving Iyar because Gabar's meek tones disassembled Iyar's raucous voice.

Iyar glowered at Naphtali. "Put up your sword, boy. Prepare a place. They are our guests. Give them my best pillows. Except for the cushion from Edrei."

Iyar's restless breathing awakened him. Judging by the fading moonlight peeping through the tent's opening, dawn would come soon. Were Gabar and his companions still lined like palm trunks on the other side of the large tent, a golden haze emanating from them? Iyar sat up against his pillows to see.

"Naphtali!"

The slave groaned.

"Naphtali!"

The boy scrambled awake. "My lord."

"They fled."

"Who?"

"The four horsemen."

Where Gabar and his companions had slept the night before, only folded blankets and stacked pillows remained.

Naphtali whistled in wonder. "We never heard a footstep."Iyar and Naphtali bolted outside, and at Naphtali's shout, the hired soldiers also rushed from their tents. In every direction, the horsemen and their steeds hadn't left a single sand print.

Naphtali, holding his dagger, swayed on the balls of his feet. "Apparitions. Last night was a visitation, my lord."

"It was a rude one," Iyar said. "The four horsemen ate a meal, then vanished without a farewell. My worst guests leave me a gift of appreciation."

"They live among the gods," Naphtali said. "They don't thank mortals."

"Then even gods lie," Iyar said. "They sought an unknown recompense. Check our goods."

Naphtali and the soldiers examined the four carts and their horses. When Naphtali returned to stand near Iyar, the boy tugged at his tunic. "My lord. The men found everything intact."

"Then go, go." Iyar shooed away the moping soldiers who hovered near Naphtali and appeared as perplexed as Iyar felt. The merchant marched inside and fumbled through his garments, tossing them into the air.

"By every cockroach in the City of Kings, where is my sash? The purple with the gold stripe. I paid dearly to own it."

Naphtali trailed behind him, still twisting his tunic.

"Do you have an itch?" Iyar's voice gurgled with anger.

"No, my lord. Look beneath your bed pillow for the sash," Naphtali pushed back a longish curl falling on his forehead. "My lord, tell me. How did Gabar and his companions escape?"

Iyar found the sash and strapped it around his waist. "We did not imprison them."

"How did they get away without us knowing it? They couldn't have drugged us. I prepared the lamb. You served the bread and wine. They must be gods."

Iyar knotted the sash, wishing he could explain how four men fled undetected in the open desert. It was that way with the night arts. The unexplainable appeared from desert to date forest, and Iyar never tired of pondering the incredible. Yissack's stories gave him that appetite years ago. But Iyar refused to indulge Naphtali now.

"A mystery," Iyar said. "Leave it at that, lest it tangle your thoughts unnecessarily. The lamb was greasier than usual. We may have dreamed it all."

"I will improve." Naphtali scratched his head. "They were spirits from the underworld. They arrived as the sun sank in the sky. When they spoke as one, didn't you feel the howl in the wind? Their voices alone could have buried us beneath the sand."

"Another desert mystery. We witnessed many together. Remember the sandstorm we survived?"

"I remember."

"Remember when we eluded an encampment of Zuzim? Had they seen us, we would have perished in a cave."

"Yes."

"View this the same," Iyar said. "We escaped with our lives. I still have a caravan. You and the soldiers finish packing. We must reach Chaniya by sunset and the City of Kings by the next sunset. I have goods to sell before King Shammah's wedding."

The soldiers dislodged the tent ropes and pegs while Iyar stalked the edge of their encampment as the early morning hours bloomed into soft sunlight. He drew in his breath, intentionally stilling his thoughts about the desert horsemen. And Raushanna. Once he was home, he could open his shop with new trinkets and fabric. Each sale would help him purchase a few properties he had spotted a few months ago. Perhaps he would even build another house.

"My lord!" A soldier rushed toward Iyar. He held half-hidden tablets wrapped in rough fabric beneath Iyar's tent.

"What is this?" Iyar dragged his forearm across his beard.

"We found these in the sand beneath your tent. To the west," the soldier said.

Naphtali sprinted toward them. "To the west? The sand sorcerers."

"A gift? Be grateful they took their winds and earthquakes with them," Iyar said.

Iyar yanked the dull fabric from the clay tablets. The cloth floated to the sand. "Common fare. Worthless."

"Yes, my lord," Naphtali said. "But please decipher what the tablets say."

Naphtali glided his left forefinger across the three tablets in Iyar's hands. The etchings on the first tablet caught the boy's attention.

"May I?" Naphtali said. He took the tablet and read it. "Your name. There. And there. And there. So many Iyars. Was this name sacred to your house?"

"My ancestors," Iyar replied. "Eleven generations before me bore my name. The first Iyar was born after the Great Deluge. He was the eldest. He and his wife, Hannah, named their firstborn son Iyar. Other Iyars followed. Only my father Yissak, although he was the eldest son, did not bear the name.

His father despised the tradition. But my father resumed it with my birth. How did these riders know this about my house?"

Iyar rubbed his thumb on his chin. "Why would Gabar leave me tablets about my ancestors? I'd prefer shekels for last evening's meal and lodging."

"It's a genealogy tablet, my lord," said Naphtali. "The names and dates go from the founding of Seth after the Great Deluge and on toward the birth of the City of Kings."

"Why do we need such a history? What value is it to me? The scribes barely pay me for decent robes. They cannot afford to buy ancient histories. Leave this uselessness here."

Naphtali was breathless, and he stuttered slightly. "Look, my lord."

At their feet, the fabric shifted into luminous sunset hues. Surprised, Iyar grunted. "Stunning."

"Gabar and his men wore these colors in their garments," Naphtali said. "This confirms what I said. They have left this for us. For you. What night arts did they employ to make the cloth change colors when you touched it?"

Moved by the cloth's dazzling beauty, Iyar couldn't conceal his astonishment.

"The tablets will be a loss, but the cloth will fetch a profit," he said. "I know the perfect noble family. They gloat with their color choices. The wife adores green. Can you believe it? Green. But her daughter could use this cloth as a sash or a headscarf."

Naphtali picked up the fabric. While neatly folding it, he leaned closer to scan the second tablet in Iyar's hands.

"Wait, my lord. That line. It says that on the foundation stone, hidden in the City of Kings, lies the mark of Aleph. Does Aleph have a mark? And where is the foundation stone hidden? It says these tablets reveal the truth about the ownership of the

City of the Great King. That's odd. We call our home the City of Kings. Not the city of one king. And Livnath sits as its queen, its patroness."

Iyar felt his hands tremble as he held the tablets. "Go on."

"The city has levels. They were built atop of each other in an exquisite pattern that rivals Livnath's temple. You know, my lord, my sister, Hulda, once slept among the temple's ruins to keep warm."

"Who cares if the pair of you slept in a stable? What else does it say?"

Iyar didn't bother to hide his impatience. One reason the merchant purchased Naphtali was because the boy loved to read and write, tasks Iyar deplored, along with chopping vegetables, losing a coin, and running out of wine. Iyar's sister Abigail loved tablets and stargazing in the heavens, while his youngest sibling, Eli, had cherished any time he could wield a tool or plow dirt. Iyar adored money and ease, nothing else.

Naphtali bit his lip; a lock of auburn hair bounced on his narrow forehead. "War will break out under two brutal kings who follow the seductress," he said. "When the first king to honor Aleph takes the throne, a fiercer war will occur during his reign. My lord, Kish and Aikah were brutal kings. They devoted their lives to Livnath. The only king etched on the Ten Pillars to serve Aleph is Shammah. No one else. King Shammah defeated the star-born and the Mikana about three years ago. And now there will be another war? When will Seth know peace?"

Iyar snatched the fabric and the second tablet from Naphtali. With a frown, he wrapped all three tablets in the glistening material. He calculated his fears. Before the Mikana attacked, Iyar fled the City of Kings. But Iyar's business losses exceeded his estimates, but the wealth he worked hard and long for eventually stabilized as King Shammah rebuilt the City of Kings.

"We haven't finished the first two tablets, and we haven't read the third," Naphtali said. "We must warn the king."

"Must? We answer to no one," Iyar said. "We owe no one."

"He's the savior-king, my lord. We must obey."

"Shammah is a yearling calf. I am not beholden."

Naphtali gawked. Even the boy understood the tablets would change their way of life. But Iyar cherished mortal, predictable comforts. Flowing from generation to generation unhindered and favoring his interests. Iyar avoided efforts to right wrongs or stand for moral principles because insights in commerce and wealth privileged him to sleep on a bed and not a floor and to live in a stone house rather than a mud one that could crumble with a heavy rain.

Iyar dreaded what would happen if the people learned that Aleph laid the foundation stone, and not Livnath. Distrust could lead to wildness. Tavern owners could seize the homes of noble families. Rioters could murder aristocrats in the streets. And while he cared little for Shammah and his reign, Iyar didn't want to disrupt the royal line of succession. He didn't want to introduce even the thought of war because he refused to instigate chaos.

"Do not speak of this to anyone in our caravan, Naphtali. Disobey me, and I will crush each of your bones."

CHAPTER TWO

PAST, PRESENT, AND FUTURE

I yar was a closed gate, a stoppered fountain. For a man who rattled off tales without end, who boasted about himself and ridiculed others with pleasure, his rocky silence swallowed up every bit of Naphtali's patience. He didn't know whether the discovery of the tablets angered Iyar or that Naphtali knew how to read what they said.

The soldiers also noticed Iyar's brooding and didn't offer their typical salty conversation to Iyar, rigid as a wall on the cart seat, arms folded, face grim.

Nightfall was in about an hour, and Chaniya lay ahead. Naphtali needed to know where they should lodge. When they had traveled this route months ago, they slept at the home of Iyar's rich friend.

The two men feasted to dawn, and the slaves never rested. They served every dish in Chaniya that shekels could buy, and after the men fell asleep at the table, their puffy faces flat on their plates, their hands gripping cups etched with gold pomegranates, the slaves cleared the mounds of uneaten food and wine, taking the leftovers for themselves. Naphtali pocketed the bread, molded by the household cooks into small, delicate hands and baked with rosemary.

Memories of rosemary bread prompted Naphtali to ask Iyar: "Are we staying at my lord's house this time? Should I send ahead a soldier to alert him of our arrival?"

The frozen stare and pose remained.

Naphtali tapped his thigh with his left hand while guiding the horse with his right. If he did nothing, they would ride all night, exhausting the horses and themselves. If he stopped, he couldn't go to his master's friend without permission. Iyar could beat him for that because he had warned the boy years ago to heed his personal etiquette. Master was infamous for his crudeness, but he never visited unannounced.

Naphtali spotted a patch of grass on the edge of the desert. He tightened the reins on the horses and steered the cart in that direction. The soldiers trailed behind him.

"Here." Naphtali pulled the reins, and the two horses paused with a weary stomp.

Stars lit the sky, and no moon glowed. Naphtali and the men secured the horses and carts and pitched the tents. When they finished and Naphtali had prepared mushroom soup, Iyar dismounted from the cart to join them. He gulped the soup, coughed when he scorched his throat, grabbed a wine jar, and waddled inside his tent.

One soldier ventured the question: "What upset your master? Those desert visitors are long gone."

Naphtali shrugged. "In time, he will be better. We'll leave at dawn so that we can reach the City of Kings by sunset."

Once the men started telling stories about their exploits with other nobles and tattled about their wives and mistresses, Naphtali wandered from camp. Above him glimmered *Reem*, the star of the horned bull. Bullish was a fitting description of his master, who worshipped his own stubbornness, if anything at all.

Naphtali didn't understand why his master refused to read them himself. The rich committed foolish sins. They squandered opportunities Naphtali longed for. They wasted food and wine, lived in houses that displayed every luxury, and hoarded property beyond what they needed while squeezing the poor for every shekel.

Not a day passed when Naphtali didn't feel the temptation to wound Iyar. The merchant gloated in his excesses, a satiated man who never knew fullness. He depended on Naphtali for everything, and the boy often felt like an unwilling extension of the man. Stealing Iyar's possessions loomed in the boy's mind every time he brought Iyar a plate, read a contract, or summoned a noble.

Something whisked through the tall grasses. Naphtali stopped walking. Perhaps it was a night creature scurrying to its den. Naphtali crouched. Another rustle, and he pulled out the dagger tied to his waist. A small fox he could overcome.

"Let me see your form that I may kill you," Naphtali wrung the words from his lips.

A giggle emerged from the grasses. "His words sound strange."

"Be quiet," said a second, deeper voice.

Two boys, Naphtali surmised. "Come out."

The pair, the tallest about Naphtali's age, pulled back the grasses.

"He has a dagger." The younger boy had bright green eyes and unruly, coiled hair that fanned from his head like tree leaves.

"Quiet." This was the voice of the older boy, muscular and taller than Naphtali.

He walked up to Naphtali. He smelled like figs. Maybe even garlic. "Who are you?"

"Naphtali. Slave of Iyar. Who are you?"

"You're trespassing."

"I'm not."

"You are. This is my family's land. Our farming rights reach the edge of the desert. It's Chaniyan law."

Naphtali couldn't challenge the boy's words, but he stiffened his shoulders and balled his fists.

"Step back from me."

"Step off my land."

"My sister is going to the City of Kings in a few days." The younger boy offered a wide smile.

Naphtali ignored him. He waited for the older boy to move. The older boy didn't.

"If you knew who my sister was, you would leave our land." The younger boy's voice registered a slight pout.

"Your sister means nothing to me," Naphtali said. "Boys. Come inside." Naphtali heard a woman's voice calling for them.

The younger boy scrambled away and yelled over his shoulder, "If you knew who my sister was, you would care."

The older boy didn't move. Neither did Naphtali.

"Boys, come home now!"

The older boy stepped back. "You don't want to see me again."

"I don't." Naphtali stepped forward.

The older boy turned and raced behind the younger boy. Naphtali assumed they were brothers. He'd never had a brother, only a sister. The push of boyhood strength affected him like a tonic. He gazed at the *Reem* in the sky. Like his master, Iyar, bullishness ran through his blood.

Naphtali took his time returning to camp. No doubt his master had fallen asleep, having gone to bed with a wine jar. Maybe his master spoke to the wine jar because he said not a word to anyone else. He found an open patch where the grasses weren't as high. He craned his neck upward from where he sat on the ground to study the *Reem*, wondering how the priests connected the star to a wild ox.

"If only I had more time to study," Naphtali said, pulling a handful of dates from his pouch.

As he chewed, he heard a woman praying: "Lord Aleph, what a night sky you have prepared for me."

Naphtali kneeled in the grasses, trying not to be seen while searching for whoever walked nearby. The woman stared skyward. Maybe she was curious about the *Reem* too.

"Thank you, Lord Aleph," the woman said. "You are a shepherd to me."

Her voice trailed off as desert breezes bent the stalks of grass. "Because of you, I have all I need. You blessed me, and my enemies bore witness. I entrust you with all that comes. I give you my husband. How I love him. How I adore and worship you. I give you my children. I give you my children's children and their descendants."

Naphtali couldn't see the woman's face, only her form in shadow. Her voice flowed over him like oil, and he imagined basking in the sound of it. He lay down and listened to her as he saw a circling light, like glittering sand, encircling the woman. The light assumed the shapes of women and men who carried cups and platters to serve her.

But the woman couldn't see them. Naphtali knew this because the women and men increased in size as she uttered supplication. "I feel your goodness. Your graciousness exceeds the goodness of earthly kings."

Naphtali jumped up to urge her to see the people surrounding her, but they smiled and motioned for the boy to be seated and stay silent.

When they finished, a feast lay before the woman. Everything sparkled, and the figures rose skyward in a radiant light.

The next day, when the gates of the City of Kings loomed on the horizon, Naphtali tried to nudge Iyar into a conversation about what he witnessed the night before in Chaniya.

"The desert was full of mystery during this caravan, my lord," Naphtali said.

He waited to see whether the stern Iyar would soften, but the merchant didn't flap an arm. Naphtali tried again.

"I saw two boys, a woman, and apparitions near our caravan. They brought cups and platters to the woman. I wonder who she is."

Iyar crowed with grim mirth. "Memories of the Chaniyan rosemary bread you love, and I loathe, stirred your stomach and fanciful thoughts."

Naphtali offered an uneasy chuckle. "Perhaps. But the woman never ate from the cups and platters. What they carried to her, I don't know."

"A waste of utensils."

"Delicacies unseen," Naphtali said.

The noisy, hurried pace of horses, carts, and people at the open gates grew louder. They were almost home. Iyar straightened on the cart as his acerbic humor returned.

"Forget your desert apparitions, Naphtali. They have melted into the sun like dregs of wine. Are we not safe within the formidable walls of the City of Kings?"

Once Iyar reached the home he built, he stored the tablets in a personal chamber cabinet and instructed Naphtali to pay the soldiers and prepare goods for sale. Meanwhile, driven by an insistent desire, Iyar walked to his family's ancestral home in the city's western section.

Memories inundated his thoughts in the late afternoon light. His mother peering out the eastern window during winter mornings and sharing eggs and gossip with a neighbor on spring afternoons. He and his siblings making sure a pot of fresh water sat on the threshold for Father to wash when he returned from hours of selling and repairing textiles.

After flames whipped through the house, and after his mother died, Iyar sought peace by tilling a garden on the seared grounds. Iyar placed his hands on the largest date palm, the first he planted.

The date palms outlasted the warring Mikana and Livnath's furious marching when she embodied her temple statue after Shammah's disastrous nuptials with Mahalath. The date palms, along with olive trees, flowers, and vegetables that grew within the garden, burst with life while Livnath's temple, where hundreds once worshipped, lay in ruins a short stroll away.

Abigail never forgave Iyar for abandoning the seared grounds of their ancestral home. She accused him of forsaking their family inheritance like an ungrateful son, and he called her selfish and short-sighted as he ordered slaves to plant the garden at once immediately after the fire.

To underscore his point, Iyar sent Abigail part of the garden's profits when the harvest was full. It was his right as the firstborn son to do as he pleased with the land. Iyar dragged his hands from the date palm. It was still his right.

A speckled dog dashed toward Iyar and sniffed his leg. Iyar wondered for a moment why the dog came to him and not to the child trailing his mother not far from him or the young man carrying barley toward the bazaar.

Then Iyar understood. Following the dog was the shopkeeper, the eccentric man who sold Naphtali to Iyar. Since their meeting two years ago, more lines grooved the man's forehead, nose, and jaw, and his bulging knees, peeking beneath the fringe of his tunic, scraped bone.

"I never heard your name," Iyar said. "Even the deaf, however, remember your creaking knees."

"They have toiled in many places. How is Naphtali?"

"Growing. More quick-witted than I ever was at that age."

The shopkeeper eased his limbs onto a rotting wooden bench. The dog curled near his feet, and for a moment, Iyar wondered if they had sat here before. Iyar's father, Yissack, read tablets from here. Odd, that like the date palm and the olive trees, the bench survived the fire.

"Quick-witted, heh?" the man said. "You presuppose Naphtali's revenge against you one day. It is the worry of tyrants. They fear the ox-whip flying from their fists and finding their backs."

Iyar didn't feel like arguing, even for amusement. Besides, the man seemed frail enough to topple from the bench with his next breath. "Your shop isn't far from here, is it?"

"I claim every part of the City of Kings."

"Without property transactions on tablets, you claim nothing but hallucinations."

"Histories do not matter to you, do they? They are not as profitable as textiles, slaves, or debt collection. Histories belong in the bloodless, dead hands of those in the underworld. But I am old enough to know that is not true. Past, present, and future mingle in the same place."

Iyar refused to argue. Nearness to his family home filled him with rare benevolence. "Maybe I know what you mean by that. This garden. This place. Even this bench. My home was here long ago, and it feels like home so many decades later."

"You remember the walls and the floors, as if they still stood," the shopkeeper said. "You hear the voices of your mother and your father and the pounding regrets of your mistakes. I told you: past, present, and future mingle in the same place."

"You sound more foreboding than the conjurers of the dead and less imaginative. The conjurers always ask for money. Will you ask me for a shekel, too, or should I summon one of my slaves to take you home?"

"Walk with me. Let's go west. It lies closer to the center of the city where I live. This courtesy you can afford. After all, I gave you a gift in Naphtali."

Iyar helped the man stand. "I purchased him, remember?"

"A trivial mention. Naphtali solves problems you cannot resolve alone."

"If he could be more consistent, I would agree with you. Naphtali is like a sudden storm. He helps; he hinders," Iyar said.

Watching Naphtali in the man's shop, huddled over tablets about property transactions and making notes on another tablet, had convinced Iyar to press a pile of shekels in the shop owner's hands.

Iyar tried to free his mind of his first memories of Naphtali in the same way he released the date palm in his family's garden. The past strangled Iyar's strength, inviting old torments to his present.

"You never moved your shop after the priests allowed Livnath's temple to fall into disarray," Iyar said.

"I stay near the temple for all the people who come hoping that Livnath will restore it to its former grandeur," the man said. "When they reach the ruins, they seek comfort."

They neared Livnath's temple site.

"Before you owned the shop, were you a priest for the goddess?" Iyar asked.

"Never."

"Then why console her followers?"

"Origins. Our oral history describes life after the Great Deluge. Our people fought to survive and to follow the Existing One. Can you imagine life after destruction? They came from a place, and they fought to get here after the Great Deluge. The lying and the unbelieving attacked them then, and they yearned to claw at their descendants. I ease their distress because there must and will be a remnant of people who stand with King Shammah when the lying and the unbelieving return."

Shepherds herded their donkeys, and children chased chickens in the distance, but no one walked where Iyar and the man stood at the bazaar's edge. The dog ran to a sloping building constructed of mud and reeds. Only the sapphire-hued door gave the structure any color.

"Is this your shop? I do not remember it after all. Or is it different?"

"Your sight has improved, not the location."

"I do not understand."

"Goodbye, Lord Iyar. Go to the opulent residence you now call home."

The man, with the dog in step with him, slammed the door on the structure, which resembled a house more than a shop, and loneliness slammed into Iyar. Sparring with the man didn't satisfy him. No one waited at Iyar's house to share a meal. Feeling isolated, Iyar shrugged off the sensation and turned away.

When he did, before him rose a glistening, transparent structure, its edges lined in blue. The square structure pushed skyward, reaching for the clouds and sun. The building stretched toward the garden of Iyar's ancestral home facing east and to the ruins of Livnath's temple facing west. The building swelled the way a man exhaled a long breath.

Iyar rubbed his forehead. He reached for his dagger, preparing himself for a feverish priest or seer to charge toward him. "What night arts are these?"

Seeking protection, Iyar pressed his back against the shopkeeper's door. When the door opened, Iyar almost fell inside.

"Aleph permitted you to witness truth," the shopkeeper said. "Heed the revelation."

"Riddles."

"Aleph inscribed life on the tablets."

"How do you know about the tablets?"

"The structure you saw is 500 by 500 cubits. It belongs here. On this site. On Livnath's temple ruins. Livnath strives to hide the unseen world from those in the seen."

"Livnath need not wrestle with me."

"She must. She will. Livnath acknowledges what you refuse to believe."

"Pigs and rats. I asked for none of this."

"Return tomorrow."

Iyar turned his back on the shopkeeper. The building was still there, pulsating and shifting toward him with fiery edges. He remembered the flames that spouted from the nostrils of the horses Gabar and his men rode.

Within the structure, he glimpsed sloshing water and an enormous, gilded cup that poured eastward. The splashing sounded like rolling waves of water that could bathe three-thousand men.

Iyar feared fire and water would consume him.

So, he ran.

Squeezed onto the shelf were small bottles. They contained herbs for stomach aches and ointments for aching knees, along with powders for indigestion and sneezes. One sealed jar caught Chazon's attention. The amber contents glowed within it.

The priest wrapped his right hand around the jar. This was the last of the elixir he and Tamiym, along with Shammah's soldiers, used to rescue the City of Kings from the Mikana. Aleph showed Chazon what herbs to combine, a mixture that defied the ways of men. Lavender, balsam, powdered palm leaves, overripe dates, onions, and licorice weren't weapons, but Chazon suspected a potent, hidden ingredient Aleph never revealed.

The jar remained on the shelf, a memorial for those rapid-fire days of war, when the Mikana scourged Seth, intent on destroying everything King Aikah had built and everything his adopted son, Shammah, stood to inherit.

Chazon stumbled into creating a small apothecary near the palace, but now it seemed natural to keep a few remedies. Shammah distrusted the royal physicians Aikah hired and assigned them to care for the sick and work under Chazon's watchful guidance.

Someone tapped on the priest's door. Chazon didn't want to answer. Much had to be done after Shammah became king, and now that he was marrying for love, Chazon longed for quiet. He planned to pilgrimage to Mount Aleph in a few days after the king wed to strengthen himself in solitude.

In a brisk gesture, Chazon swung open his door. "Yes?"

A squat man in worn robes hovered at the threshold, his head bent, with ears protruding like wheels. "Priest of Aleph. I heard you have food."

For a moment, Chazon hesitated because he knew Shammah established feeding centers that remained open day and night. Families could sup at the tables if their crops failed, or sickness plagued them.

Before Chazon could reply, the man explained. "We traveled from Edrei and were told to come to you. The feeding centers have run out."

"Of course. Wait here."

He turned to go to his small oven, but after thinking about it, pivoted to ask the man's name. The man disappeared. Chazon stepped into the street. No one was there.

The priest frowned, pressing his heavy, steel-gray eyebrows together. When he returned to his apothecary, the window was open. Someone stole the sealed jar. The other jars stood untouched. Chazon willed himself not to be alarmed. Whoever took the jar knew what they wanted and where it was.

Another knock, then another. Chazon went to the door, ready to summon fire. Had the squat man returned to see whether his ruse with an accomplice worked?

Chazon yanked open the door. "Return my potion!"

He swallowed. Before him were King Shammah and his personal guards, the Shamgar. A few neighborhood children and their mothers trailed behind them, intrigued by the unexpected royal visit to this part of the City of Kings.

Chazon bowed in apology. "My lord!"

Shammah grinned. "Chasing away innocent children as you did me, priest? What rebellion do you judge them for?"

The king entered without asking, preoccupied, ready to talk, rubbing his beard as if insight would emerge from each stroke.

Chazon leaned against a wall to calm his emotions. He hadn't expected the king and not here in these quarters. The priest would resolve the theft when the king departed. Alerting Shammah would enlarge a minor problem.

"Dare I be so happy, Chazon? Joy overflows, and yet, I wonder at its simple glory. Love holds a heart and never releases it. I am a happy prisoner, and I will never be free."

The king appeared nervous, yet full of hope, a man in love. Even the somber-faced Shamgar, smiled in bemusement.

"Love is a gift from Aleph because the Existing One is love, the spring that feeds the river, the sky that seeds the rain," Chazon said.

Shammah paced, hands on hips. "My thoughts roam in the present and dash to the future. Always, Tamiym is there. I sense Aleph's pleasure at the union, a sunlight that doesn't dim. But the joy, the joy. Its weight overwhelms me."

The king paused in the center of the room. "Lavender. Freshly cut."

"I placed blooms in the back room."

"Ah. Calming. Very calming." Shammah resumed his pacing. "I have sequestered myself, and yet I could not stay alone anymore. So, I came to you. How can I say? Ruling with Tamiym fills me with sweet expectations. Then, in the next moment, I dread bringing her to the palace. Chaniya and her family fill her with happiness and peace. Why should I disrupt that by offering her a place alongside me as a new queen? I can't predict the difficulties that lie ahead. People ignite disputes like cockroaches snare street crumbs. Pretense from Livnath's priests remains fixed as the stars hanging above us. They lust to revive their temple and claim ownership of the city. At every feast, the nobles wager on my failure. The soldiers worry about another war, and I can't ease the needs of the poor quickly enough. But, ah, all I want. . ."

"My lord. Tamiym accepted your marriage promise and your throne. She chose to be your queen."

"She did, didn't she?"

"You chose a matchless bride."

Shammah's gaze fell on the rose blooms, stretching through a window from outside. He walked over and traced their petals with his right thumb. A few children gathered to glimpse the king, and Shammah rewarded them with a smile and roses.

"My lord, I need those blooms." Chazon folded his arms in annoyance and worry. *Who was the thief and how did they know about the sealed jar? Why had he brought the jar here?* The neighborhood was a bustling one, a rare place where aristocrat, scribe, merchant, farmer, slave, and laborer lived. The area seemed the perfect place where he could live undetected as he mingled among neighbors.

"Be generous, Chazon. I will plant more roses for you," Shammah said. "In fact, I order you to arrange for gardens to be planted in this sector of the city. Speak with the families here about it. Listen to their proposals. Then come see me after a reasonable time following my wedding."

Shammah pressed a few roses into the hands of another child before facing the priest. "All I want is to invite our people to explore the truths of Aleph and rule in peace with Tamiym beside me."

"Peace is a natural desire. Continue to ask Aleph to build peace in the foundations of your marriage and reign. But do not doubt Aleph's wisdom in this. Never trail after false peace when authentic peace comes with difficulty, even war. The Existing One extracts beauty from struggle. If Aleph leads you to the mountain of destiny, I pray you do not flee its cliffs."

Shammah resembled the boy who once hounded Chazon with questions about battles, stars, histories, and mysteries. With every question he asked, Chazon tried to answer with love.

"My lord?" Chazon asked. "You are silent."

"Who can prepare for a future covered by mist? I cannot think of a sword or spear in the palace arsenal that can protect the throne from the unknown. Aleph's sword is all I have or need. Your wisdom would tell me this."

"Consider it said."

Shammah sat on a stool with a thud. The wide grin returned, replacing the melancholy. "What were you doing when I arrived? I know that frown, deeper and more ferocious than all others. Are you hiding something? You master your worry and bring it to heel, reining in its agonies, a sea monster subdued. As Peleg and I fled the Water People, Aleph used your face to strengthen me. Tell the king. Tell your friend. What anxiety haunts you?"

Shammah shooed the Shamgar from the room and sat on the stool, tapping his fingers on his knees, ready to listen.

Chazon lowered his head and tucked his hands behind his back, a familiar pose to help him think and parse his words with care. Two choices unfolded before him: lie to the king, which was punishable by death or prison, or share suspicions about Seth's enemies instigating a war by stealing the sealed jar from Chazon's apothecary.

The priest spurned presenting news of potential war as a wedding gift only hours before the king's nuptials. Any act that could spoil Shammah's joy repelled him.

"Has the fragrance of lavender caused you to slumber? It is midday," Shammah said.

Chazon twisted his tunic belt. *War.* He remembered the women who lifted fallen soldiers and dug through heaps of rubble to find their husbands, sons, and brothers during the bloodshed under King Aikah's reign. Thoughts of Shammah facing battle again so soon after the Great War fell like blows. *How could I lose him,* Chazon thought.

He protected the studious and mournful boy who had lost his parents because of Aikah's warring, and Chazon wanted to shield Shammah now, only hours before his royal wedding.

Shammah stood, shoving away the stool. Eager questioning shifted into imperiousness. "You hide something from the king. What is it?"

The priest nodded. The words of the lie in Chazon's heart curdled like milk.

"My lord," he began.

Peleg charged through the door with a broad grin. Chazon had never seen Shammah's friend so gleeful. "My king! There you are. It took a lot to persuade the Shamgar to allow me inside, and it took a lot for me to do this."

He pointed to the people gathering outside alongside a painted cart. "You pledged allegiance to Aleph, so I invited followers of that gloomy deity to present you to the City of Kings before the wedding. Aikah rode through the City of Kings before he married Queen Gila at Livnath's temple. The ruins are dreadful right now.

"Anyway, I thought maybe you could ride before your people in the City of Kings and then back to the palace. Aleph doesn't have a temple or anything, but I can't change that, can I?"

Shammah dragged an arm around Peleg's shoulders. "You view the work of the Existing One as gloomy, and yet Aleph labors through your hands."

"You don't mind?" PPeleg's voice rose. "I didn't place a gambling bet on this. I pledge that to you."

"It pleases me," Shammah said.

Peleg faced Chazon. "I'm sorry, my lord, for not alerting you as the priest of Aleph. Something stirred me to arrange the royal presentation and invite followers of Aleph to celebrate their king. It's a spontaneous gesture, but it doesn't violate your creed, does it?"

"You did well, Peleg," Chazon's voice was weak. "You redeemed what was almost lost."

Peleg guided Shammah outside. The king hugged adults, lifted toddlers to his shoulders, and accepted blooms and modest gifts of food and embroidered fabrics. Shammah got into the cart while the people danced around him with songs.

"Aleph's king for the City of Kings," the people chanted.

Chazon turned away. Inside, he collapsed before the jars on the shelves. The window remained open. Then the priest wept because what he dreaded was beginning.

⌐~⌐~⌐

Iyar mocked himself for going, but he returned to the shopkeeper's house the next morning. Like yesterday, he didn't take Naphtali or any of the slaves, which wasn't his usual manner. But if this were going to be a foolhardy visit, Iyar chose humiliation without witnesses.

No one answered the shopkeeper's sapphire-hued door. Iyar didn't think it was unusual because the man, despite his noisy knees, would often appear like smoke, an unrestrained traveler in the City of Kings.

When Iyar tired of knocking on the man's door, he left. He strolled past Livnath's ruined temple and noticed a flicker of activity.

Strutting so that passersby could see them in the bazaar area, architects and builders measured the temple's foundation. Iyar watched, stunned. For three years, Livnath's priests had shied away from the site as if the ground itself spurned them.

But now, a day after Iyar glimpsed the massive, unearthly structure in front of the shopkeeper's house, Livnath's devotees were preparing to restore the temple.

In a concept foreign to him, Iyar felt as if Livnath herself resisted his curiosity about the ruins. He remembered what the man told him: *Livnath strives to hide the unseen world from those in the seen.* Iyar waited in a nearby tavern until the architect and builders finished their measurements. After two cups of beer, Iyar moved with random steps through the ruins of Livnath's temple. A man treading through an open tomb.

Charred clay bricks and a few blocks of stone clustered in heaps provided the only evidence of the rituals for Livnath. The building had suffered damage during the fires the Mikana set when they torched the building during the Great War. Priests had pulled the silver and gold wall hangings from the walls and taken the furnishings to their homes.

At one time, the statue of the moon goddess stood at the center of the structure. After Shammah recaptured the city, the spirit of Livnath filled the statue and marched it from the temple, carrying Shammah's bride, Mahalath, on their wedding day outside the walls of the City of Kings. Once beyond the city gate, the statue disappeared in a ring of clouds. No one saw Mahalath again.

Iyar often wondered why his grand house survived the Great War while an unexpected blaze destroyed his ancestral home within a night. His mother was inconsolable. The home was her last tie to their father, and she felt she had cut them off from the family line, although it wasn't her fault. The fire had raged suddenly in the drought months of Seth, and they couldn't find enough water to subdue the flames.

He remembered being about ten or twelve years old when he slipped into one of the temple's shadowed corners and observed screeching priests and dancing priestesses as they slung incense and slew lambs and calves. Iyar ran home and told his father about what he saw, and his father's quick reaction startled him.

Yissack shook his son's shoulders. "Never go there again, Iyar. Do you hear me? It is not the place for my son and heir."

Iyar attempted to wriggle from his father's grip, but Yissack tightened his hold. "You are my eldest, and I love you, but if you return to that dreadful place again, my chastisement will be severe."

Iyar thought his father intended to deter him from roaming the city unescorted. Boys and girls sometimes went missing in the City of Kings, and anguished parents worried whether the star-born snatched their children or forced them into Livnath's priesthood before carrying them to other cities in Seth or, at worst, far from the kingdom.

Iyar considered the three tablets Gabar left in his care. There had to be more that drove his father to insist that Iyar never return to the temple.

Meditating on the past ended. Again, Iyar heard the shopkeeper's knees first. The man creaked a path from behind him.

"Are you believing at last?" The man huffed as he stood before Iyar.

"Why are you a stealthy visitor? I don't know whether to minister ointment to your knees or pull out my dagger. Your steps can be mistaken as my friend or enemy."

"Friend, always friend."

"Friends share birth names," Iyar said. "Do you not have a mother, a father? Are you not someone's offspring? Tell me the name your parents gave you."

The shopkeeper ignored Iyar's words with a grunt and a growl. "Remember, I told you yesterday. Livnath seeks to hide the unseen by building another frightful temple tower, each stone emboldened by terrible hate.

"Distractions and the night-arts saw, chisel, and knife through the lives of the innocent in Livnath's hands. She and the other star-born pummel into this realm, trying to erect towers of terror to oppress or kill us. A friend will tell you that."

"Such a friend I would dispatch to an enemy to steal their peace instead of mine. It does not comfort me."

"Livnath's tower will take years to rebuild, but the priests must never finish," the shopkeeper said. "It must never soar to the stars again, and you must devise a way to halt its progress."

"You are a soothsayer who labors for souls," Iyar said. His irritation grew. "Your house with its blue door seduces needy men and women who cannot direct their lives beyond their fingertips. My mother did not birth me to interrupt construction projects. I offer loans for the temple's construction because I was born to multiply shekels. Builders need land. They need stone. They need wood. They need water. They need camels, donkeys, and horses. They need slaves. They need money.

"I manipulate people. I create events that enable me to expand my wealth. Though I doubt they have skills of commerce at all, I will provide a fair inheritance for those faithless offspring of mine. It is what my father would expect me to do."

The man clucked his tongue. "What else must I do to persuade you, Iyar? A babe who has never cooed his mother's name would comprehend what you reject. The weight of your family's history rides your shoulders. Until you right yourself, you are of no use to anyone."

Iyar reached his house. Slaves helped him shed his dusty cloak. They offered him water. Then wine. It was wine from Yaphah, the wine of lazy fishermen and nomadic sailors. He had consumed all the Midvar wine except the jar he intended as a gift for the royal nuptials.

Iyar threw his frustration about the lack of Midvar wine into his bellowing voice.

"Where is Naphtali?"

"Sleeping, my lord," a slave said.

"Ease for the undeserving and useless."

"My lord?" The slave searched his face.

Pushing the slave away, Iyar rushed to the rooftop and peered down the narrow street. Was the sapphire building still there, heaving like a man on fire?

The structure had disappeared.

Iyar stomped back to his chambers and pulled the tablets from the cabinet. The fabric glistened in his hands as he unwrapped them.

With a pout, he forced himself to read the symbols, going from right to left, realizing he had read little beyond commerce and building tablets since the scribes hammered knowledge into him, a distracted boy.

"As snakes rustle in the grass," Iyar said as he started the first tablet about his ancestor Iyar and that man's firstborn son, also named Iyar. The time was before the people built the City of Kings on a lush plain where the first families settled after the Great Deluge.

Iyar sat on his haunches. "Naphtali was right. This is my family's story. Should I not know it?"

CHAPTER THREE

WOOED BY THE MOON

After the Great Deluge, generations were born again. The elders wandered from the desolate mountain places until they found a new home, a land filled with date palms, fruits and vegetables, marshes and rivers, and mountains and deserts.

At least, that's what the second Iyar's father told him happened. His father, the very first Iyar of their house, said that as the first-born, he was old enough to understand. Iyar didn't feel old enough for anything except catching a larger barbel than Zetham and lounging along the shores of the Time Sea, waiting for the fish to slip into their net. Nothing mattered more.

Zetham unknotted the net. "You're doing it again."

"I don't know what you mean."

"Mother says your face clouds when you mumble to yourself."

"I didn't mumble."

"Yes, you did. I caught you. Mumble, mumble, mumble."

Iyar pulled the net closer to him. "Foolish one. I catch fish better than you."

The net shook. Three large barbels wiggled within the net. They weren't larger than Zetham, but they were huge: three hefty meals for the family to share.

Before Iyar could focus his full attention on the net, he glimpsed a young woman kneeling to cup water. He gripped the tossing net, studying her at the same time. Noonday sun threaded her brown-gold hair, which fell into curly tendrils dripping along her back.

"Who is she?"

Zetham struggled to hold the net. "Don't lose the fish, Iyar."

"Mother says they are for tonight." Iyar looked upward. "I've not seen her in the village. She looks like no one I've ever seen, even Mother. And Mother is beautiful."

Net in hand, Iyar snatched another look. The woman jerked her leg, jamming her ankle between the rocks. Iyar struggled about what to do. Father often chided him for not showing more compassion toward the poor or the grieving. The woman appeared neither poor nor grieving, but she needed help.

"She's trapped," Iyar said.

"The fish can't move either. Hold on, Iyar."

Iyar and Zetham hauled the net up with a heave. They slapped the net on the shore, fell back on their haunches, gasping for air. The tossing fish near them fought to live.

Iyar stood. "Now let's help her."

When the boys reached the woman, they stepped back. A retching sensation climbed into Iyar's throat. He swallowed hard, then pulled Zetham to his side. "Quiet."

Iyar's whisper was harsh, but it had the intended effect: the younger boy put his hand over his mouth, preventing a howl of surprise.

From where they were fishing, they saw the woman's hair and form. Iyar thought she was in her teens. Before them stood an aged woman with a face gray as stagnant water. Ages had plowed grimy wrinkles into her skin. The wrinkles deepened as the boys stared. The fragrance of rotten meat also surrounded her, and Zetham kept coughing because of the odor and because he couldn't help laughing. Iyar nudged him. His brother could be cruel and thoughtless. Both could do better.

"Can you help me?" The woman's voice danced in their ears.

Iyar noticed she stood upright; her bare ankles unscathed.

"You're no longer trapped."

"I still need you." The melody underlying her voice was too much for Iyar to bear.

Swaying, he moved forward. "We can call our mother. She's not far away from here. She can give you food or take you back to your people if you're lost."

"I'm not lost. You found me, Iyar. Because you did, I will reward you with treasures. By the next moon, when you reach home, I will come to you. I will tell you what I need."

"How do you know my name? How do you know we're only visiting relatives in Yaphah?"

When she caressed Iyar's cheek, the shade of wet branches and slightly rough with newborn stubble, he collapsed, eyes wide open.

The woman's ancient face glowed silver. "Look for the moon."

In less than three weeks, the moon hung over Ariel where they lived. Iyar didn't want to see the woman again. She wooed and repelled. Iyar felt queasy when moonlight crept onto the balcony. Gripping his stomach, he brought his knees to his chest.

On the other bed, Zetham groaned. "They're ugly. Huge. Every time I fall asleep, I see them."

"Ignore them. Don't leave your bed."

"I'm calling Mother."

"We must protect Mother from this woman. Let her stay with Sister."

"She's a babe. She sleeps. I need Mother. So do you."

"Be silent and stay in bed."

Moonlight soared into their room like a spear. They heard humming. It was her. Her voice tinkled like drops of water.

A spasm ripped through Iyar's belly. "Don't answer her."

The humming grew louder and hovered over them. The room felt hot.

"Please, Brother. I can't stop them. They're biting me."

Finally, the boys stumbled from bed. Once they stood on the balcony, Zetham's fears fled. Iyar's sickness stopped.

The nameless woman greeted them from a shadowed corner of the balcony. More creases marred her face. "You've missed me."

If possible, Iyar thought, her voice sounded even sweeter than it did by the river.

She reached out to touch Iyar again. Zetham blocked her, his sky-blue eyes glinting. "Do not hurt him. He slept for days the last time we met. I thought him near death."

The woman caressed Zetham's jaw until he swooned.

"Now both of you will love me."

Iyar reached Zetham before he fell. "Have you hurt him?"

"Did I injure you?"

"I know not—only that my soul cannot resist."

The old woman giggled like a girl before she swung her shoulders back with a sudden sternness. She moved closer to Iyar. "Go to your father's room. Retrieve the tablets in his cabinet. I want to borrow them. Your mother rests in your sister's chamber so you will not wake her. Once you have the tablets, return to me."

Iyar wasn't going to leave his brother with the woman, so he dragged the lethargic Zetham with him. Once inside the room where his parents slept, Iyar placed Zetham on a stool.

A sparkling cloth encased the tablets lying in Father's cabinet.

They weren't too heavy. Fear kept him from opening the cloth to look at them or count them.

Iyar longed for Father, who received the tablets from the elders during a ceremony at Mount Aleph. The way Iyar understood it, the elders expected Father to guard the tablets until they completed the altar. Beneath it, the elders planned to bury the tablets in baked brick boxes. What Iyar didn't understand was why the woman wanted them.

He didn't realize he had spoken out loud until he heard a murmur from Zetham.

"Perhaps she's an elder too." Zetham shook his head, trying to diffuse the lingering drowsiness from the woman's touch.

"Then why not ask Father for them? Why come to me?"

"Let's ask her."

"Right. There must be a reason."

The boys left their parents' quarters. Iyar carried the tablets close to his chest.

When he reached the woman, he inserted as much authority into his voice as he could muster. "Are you an elder? They asked my father to keep them safe until the elders built Aleph's altar. Reassure us you will act in the will of our father."

"You have found me out. I know your father is away. Otherwise, I would ask him. I knew I could trust the firstborn of Iyar to help me as their father has helped me in the past."

"My father has helped you?" Iyar couldn't think of a single reason why his father would help her.

"Many times. And you are so like your namesake. I see why you share his name. Strong. Trustworthy. Protective."

"I am?"

"I am like father too." Zetham's drowsy tone revealed that his brother listened but didn't comprehend what was happening. The woman took a demure step, fixing her gaze on them while reaching out to the tablets with tapered hands. Brown spots marked her pale skin.

Iyar hugged the tablets closer to his chest. He felt like he was climbing a mountain.

The woman smiled. "You both are Iyar's dear sons. I see why he talks with pride about you to the elders. Strong. Trustworthy. Protective."

"You said that before." Iyar's tone was curt, but the thought of Father bragging about his sons left Iyar bemused. Whenever the elder Iyar praised him, sunlight drenched Iyar. A punishing hand from Father, however, left Iyar soaked with pain.

Iyar's grip on the tablets loosened for a moment.

It was just enough.

The woman seized the tablets and held them to her face. The wrinkles and the haunted expression dissolved into the unlined face of a young woman. The brown-gold curls he once saw returned.

"Thank you, firstborn son of Iyar. What treasure you have given me. Treasure, I will return to you."

She twinkled a smile at Zetham. "You too."

Rage consumed their home when Father returned. He lined the boys in front of him, holding bundled branches, ready to beat them. Iyar stiffened his body, bracing his body for pain.

A few branches would sting, but a bundle of sticks and thorns would draw blood.

"You rummaged through my things for the goddess of the moon? You disrupted the peace of our people because she was beautiful, then she was horrifying? My shame will never end."

Iyar watched his father raise his hand. Hearing his brother cry, Iyar wrapped a reassuring arm around Zetham, who was crying.

As they bent their heads, ready for blows, Mother flung herself between them.

"Iyar, no."

"They have shamed me. They have shamed us. How can I face the elders? Aleph appointed our family to care for the tablets. Do you hear me, Hannah? Appointed."

"We have not lost everything. I know a way to redeem our house."

"How? Our sons destroyed our honor."

"Trust me, beloved. There is a way."

"Do you not fear Aleph?"

"I do. But you fear the elders more."

The elder Iyar glared at his wife and sons before stalking from the room, the branches clumped in his right fist.

Hannah hugged Iyar and Zetham. "Stay with each other."

When she left the room, Iyar and Zetham slumped to the floor.

"I have never seen Father so angry," Zetham said. "Had he struck us, we would have worn healing cloths for weeks."

Iyar nodded but said nothing. Though Father hadn't hit them, imagining the welts and blood silenced him. He and Zetham listened as their parents argued in the courtyard.

Father was the loudest, and Iyar suspected fear crawled beneath his father's biting words.

Zetham fidgeted on his stool. "Father thinks the elders will not forgive him and worries we will lose all we have. What will happen to us, Iyar? Maybe the lady will give the tablets back."

"We were wrong," the Iyar said at last. "I was wrong most of all. I was wrong to take something entrusted to Father. As the firstborn of my father, how can he face the elders of the Existing One? I have betrayed our people."

Zetham placed his small hand on his brother's. "Peace. Mother will get the tablets back."

Iyar shook himself from Zetham. "I need water. You wait for Mother."

While his father and mother quarreled downstairs, Iyar went to the balcony where he and Zetham had greeted the moon. He hung his head. She wasn't beautiful at the beginning when they were at the river when he thought she had caught her ankle between the rocks.

Not really. Mother was lovelier, with skin the color of ripened emmer wheat and eyes that danced with blue. The woman's manner ensnared him more than her physical appearance, and with that thought, the crushing despair returned. He understood now. A shadow summoned Iyar. Sight deceived him. He saw what he wanted to see.

As moonlight flooded from the east, Iyar pressed a damp cloth on his pupils. A howl surged from him, a boy crawling into inescapable manhood.

"My son, what have you done?" Hannah held her shivering son Iyar.

The boy writhed in her arms. "I brought shame to my house because I allowed the sight of the goddess to rule me. I don't deserve to see again, Mother. I don't. Please ask Father to forgive me."

With a face streaked with tears, Zetham watched from the shadows of the balcony. His brother's pain was his. Iyar wounded his own eyes from herbs their mother warned them never to touch. A child's rage erupted within Zetham's throat as he turned to the moon, which rose cold-white and flat. "My life, and the life of any descendants I have, and the descendants of my brother Iyar, will one day rise and curse you, moon goddess, for the horror you brought upon us. I vow this before the Mighty Aleph."

The community of elders gave Iyar a choice because of his son's betrayal. Kill his firstborn Iyar in the wilds or experience death himself. The elders demanded a sacrifice. Iyar longed for deliverance from the evil coiling around his house. The elders scrambled to act in a punitive way to deter the small but growing number of Livnath followers. Livnath already had lured boys and several men in the camp to become her priests and planned a temple tower in her honor, ignoring the families who needed reliable shelter.

To inflict more pain, and to boast before Aleph, they planned to build the temple going west to the center of the Ariel encampment, a short walk from Iyar's home. Livnath's greed for Aleph's sacred land was a potent demand her acolytes rushed to answer.

Without the tablets, the elders could not counter Livnath's claim to Ariel, the land where they settled, but they could unleash their helplessness by punishing Iyar and his family. Their dread felt as jagged as the rocks surrounding them.

"Will no one seek Aleph? Why do we presume punishment?" Hannah's pleas on behalf of her family went unanswered before the council. Men and women stood with the sun burning upon them, some turning away from Hannah's imploring face.

The men bound the elder Iyar, who licked his chapped lips. He tasted blood. Days of hunger and thirst weakened him, and he swayed. A prelude to death. A few steps away stood his blinded son with a stick to guide him. The boy trembled as if the day were cold and not hot. He mumbled nervously, causing Iyar to weep openly. His firstborn had entered manhood weaker than a babe. How would he manage? Who would protect him? He gazed at Zetham, tugging Hannah's tunic, twisting his nose and lips in anger. Rage had befriended his second son.

Iyar yearned to rescue them both, to bring them back to the paths they once walked as children. He clawed his bound hands, longing to bring a greater pain to his body to override the horror before him. Had he not become enraged? Had he comforted his sons after Livnath deceived him? Had he sought wisdom from Aleph?

He forced himself to focus on Hannah. She had aged suns and moons since Livnath snatched the tablets, and Iyar suspected his wife possessed no more tears, only an incessant groaning. Their happiness when they traveled from the east to this place seemed lifetimes away.

He scanned the crowds and searched for his boyhood friend, Patal. He and his sons had gone hunting these past weeks, searching for fresh places for a flock. Having lost his wife during their journey to Ariel, Patal didn't leave anyone home. No one from his house would witness what was happening, and that grieved Iyar, pummeling him with more loneliness.

What was happening was beyond full comprehension to Iyar, and he longed to walk until he reached the horizon and life returned to what it once was. Only a short time ago, the elders prayed blessings over him as the caretaker of the tablets, which expressed Aleph's will for the new sacred space of Ariel. They charged Iyar with protecting the tablets from Aleph's adversaries and decided that Iyar's house would be part of a temple space that to be constructed one day.

One mistake brought generations of loss. When Iyar should have been diligent to ensure the tablets' safekeeping, he was negligent. He didn't watch. He didn't guard. He didn't protect. Iyar almost fainted, rocked afresh by his error.

"Mercy, elders, mercy," Hannah said. "My boy is only a child. He has injured his own body because of his sorrow. There's no need for this, another crime to shame us all."

Tapel, the oldest of the elders, whose grandfather was among the families that first began the migration from the east once the waters receded, pointed a finger at Hannah. "Your husband, woman, is who we blame. A rebellious son is the fruit of a father's heart. Iyar, bow your head. You exposed us to Livnath's hate."

Iyar felt the weight of the elder's condemnation with each word shoveled on them.

"Do you not remember the havoc her kind wreaked before the Great Deluge?" Tapel continued. "Can you not hear the footsteps of the giants the elders warned us about? Your slothful caretaking of a gift from Aleph will imprison us in this dry area, crippling our prosperity for generations to come. Choose your punishment."

Hannah's voice rose to a raw scream. "Is not your way the ways of the giants? Have you sought the heart of Aleph, or do you presume to know it? Why not beseech Aleph in repentance and find out what the Existing One would have us to do? The moon goddess and the giants do not seek Aleph's counsel. You behave as they do. You assume Aleph's anger, yes, but do you see Aleph's mercy? Are you Aleph's hand, or are you the icy, faithless breath of Livnath?"

"We will mete out punishment, wife of the shamed Iyar. Because of your house, we slander the house of Aleph. Our people are unsafe."

Iyar knew there was no actual choice. The elders were too fearful. And fear led to reckless decisions. He held up his head with a wry expression. It was the beginning, again, for mortals, since the floodwaters receded. Blemished by the enemies of Aleph and the transgressions of his house, the Existing One would have to select another house because of his failure.

Hannah thrust her shoulders back to launch another protest, fearless before the sober elders. Though weak, Iyar called out to her. "My courageous love. Peace. My affections for you never have been greater than this moment. Our sons will care for you as their mother because we have taught them to do so."

"Help me petition Aleph, Husband. They lie. They have not sought the Existing One, and they claim to wield his will. There is a stench to their betrayal, a foulness that invades our camp. I am certain it has reached the throne of Aleph and the council."

Iyar's voice softened. "Before this assembly, and before the council above the heavens, I repent before Aleph for our house and beg the Existing One to restore our descendants. May they willingly serve the new heirs of Aleph's promises."

Tapel spat on the ground and rubbed his foot into the spittle. "May it never be. You will die in the wilds. Livnath's kind will consume you. Your son, Iyar, is blind and sickly and will never lead your house in honor. Zetham will flounder because rage springs from him like rot. Hannah will die an old and broken woman, humiliated by her husband and her sons. I decree it so."

The elders dragged Iyar far from the camp. They found a small cliff that hung over a valley. As Iyar tumbled over the sharp rocks, Hannah's wails to Aleph echoed above him, the last sounds of Earth.

CHAPTER FOUR

ONLY HUMILITY

Iyar put down the first and second tablets, nauseous. Wiping his forehead, he quickly calculated. The marks came from the beginning era of Seth, based on the pictographs. At least that much Iyar kept from scribal school long ago. Though they were old, the tablet etchings were clear. The scribes mentioned Aleph throughout the narrative and depicted the deity through the pictograph of an ox.

Livnath wasn't the patroness of Seth. She didn't create the bosom of the earth, as she claimed, and as generations of Sethite parents had taught their children from birth. Livnath the interloper seduced boys to betray their father and abandon their allegiance to Aleph.

Iyar now understood why his father Yissack shook him like a reed when he slipped into Livnath's temple, piqued by the priestly rituals. Yissack more than likely knew the story of their ancestors. While Yissack never told him about the first Iyar and the family story after the Great Deluge, that Livnath's temple intrigued Yissack's firstborn son must have unnerved him. The first two tablets were those the elders appointed the first Iyar to protect. He couldn't bear to read the third tablet. It held answers for another time. Iyar tore off his tunic, feeling overheated. From a pitcher on a table, he poured cool water on his shoulders. Abigail would know what to do and had proven that ability during their childhood when she rescued two kittens trapped beneath a cart and whispered words for him to say when Yissack disciplined him.

But Iyar couldn't go to her. She wouldn't want to hear from her older brother. He would have to find his way.

Iyar marched to a small adjoining chamber where a small lamp illuminated the deepening twilight. Naphtali lay on his stomach on the floor, snoring. Why was he always sleeping? And why did the boy snore like a full man?

"Naphtali!"

The boy jumped awake. A dagger gleamed in his right hand while he wiped his eyelids with his left.

"Are we being attacked again by pirates?"

"We will take the tablets to the king."

Sleep fell from Naphtali. He thinned his lips, as if preventing himself from questioning Iyar's sincerity.

Naphtali straightened his tunic and rose. "Are we going now? At night?"

"Do you want to know why I kept quiet?" Iyar asked.

"Does it matter? You're speaking now."

"I must not tarry."

"Who cured your blindness?"

"Rejoice at my sight."

"But have you calculated your steps? King Shammah doesn't like you. No one in the palace likes you. Crumbs of days-old bread licked by dogs receive more acclaim. Please forgive my insolence, my lord, but after you recited your fees for that poor farmer's barley loans at the council, only the nobles overlooked your unkindness."

That day before the council was one Naphtali never forgot. In a rare turn, Shammah had sat in the council. Because the king joined them, people from throughout the city pressed into the chambers. The air was hot and sticky. Iyar kept wiping his neck and jaw, and Naphtali wondered when Iyar would snap at the council members.

"My lord," Iyar had said to the council elder. "In good faith, I gave this farmer the loan he requested. Should not he return to me my 500 shekels in good faith?"

The farmer kneeled before the bench where the elders sat. "Drought struck my barley. I was too far away from other fields to share water sources. I ask for mercy, my lords, lest I forfeit my father's land and my inheritance."

"You understood the lending laws when you agreed to the contract with Lord Iyar?" an elder asked.

"Yes, my lord."

The elder nodded toward Shammah, who watched the scene with his chin in his palm. While the nobles commanded their slaves to fan them or sprinkle them with water scented with florals, the king waved his slaves away. He urged them to find shade or a cool corner and turned his attention back to the council proceedings, despite the heat, the flies, and the human sweat.

"My lord the king, do you want to rule on this?" the elder asked.

"I do." Shammah rose and planted himself before Iyar. Then he paced around the merchant, saying nothing. Naphtali remembered thinking that Shammah searched for understanding about Iyar before he eventually decided.

"For the farmer. Charge him interest for the delay, but give him more time to pay the loan so that he can rebuild," Shammah said. "For the merchant. You are Lord Iyar, correct? Son of Yissack? You will lessen your loan to the merchant by half, and the interest will match that additional fee, do you understand? If you build your wealth on the backs of the broken, upon your back I will wield justice."

Naphtali shuddered as he recalled the thunder in Shammah's voice. He didn't want his master to encounter it again. The boy touched Iyar's forearm. "My lord, you risk the king's anger. Again, I remember how he rebuked you when I joined he attended the council-court."

"Like a sailor heeding summons from across a strange sea, I accept the possibility of peril," Iyar said.

"What prompts you to talk with the king about the tablets now? It didn't matter to you before." Naphtali's stammer returned, expressing his irritation.

"I will hand over the tablets. Will that satisfy you? Your judgment is a burning hand. It is merciless."

"You have the chance to do good, my lord. A chance that requires little effort and no money."

"There is always a cost."

"Only humility."

The thought of meekness rattled Iyar, especially coming from Naphtali. Before Naphtali reached Iyar's home after being purchased as a slave, before Iyar cursed the boy for not having his robes ready quickly enough, or fumed because his meals were cold, Iyar wounded him. Naphtali pleaded with Iyar to buy his sister, and Iyar refused to heed his request. The girl was a cook. Iyar didn't need another awkward youngster in his kitchen. Every day he felt overrun by slaves, older ones he trusted but who were arrogant because of their longevity in his house or frail because of their aging bodies, and younger, unseasoned ones who struggled to hold a cup without dropping it.

But Naphtali's downcast expression led Iyar to ask one of his friends to purchase Naphtali's sister. An irritable slave dominated his friend's kitchen and, worst of all, couldn't boil vegetables without scorching them.

After his friend bought Naphtali's sister, Iyar thought he had fulfilled his obligation. But every time Naphtali became weary, his hunched walk and hounded gaze revealed how much he missed his sister. Sometimes, worn down by guilt, Iyar offhandedly encouraged the boy to visit his sister when he had finished his tasks. Whenever he could, the boy slipped away to see her.

And he always came back, even if it meant reentering the cave of Iyar's cruelties, like kicking Naphtali or demanding the slave work until a feverish weariness overtook him. Naphtali had survived these years in Iyar's household, proving himself an excellent investment and trustworthy beyond Iyar's expectations. Iyar relied more on the artless boy than his three adult children or the other forty-nine slaves serving his house.

Slaves draped the gates and walls of the City of Kings with flowers and ribbons. People already spilled in from throughout Seth to witness the marriage of King Shammah to Tamiym. Normally, Iyar engaged everyone with goods as his caravan rocked to the palace. Everyone represented a potential sale, and therefore another shekel. Now, each person represented an obstacle as he steered his cart straight to the palace and requested an audience with the king. The lieutenant greeted him with a smile but blocked him from entering.

"My lord, I know your rank allows you to request an audience with the king, but during his time of joy, we're not allowing anyone to enter the palace. Queen Tamiym will enter the City of Kings in two days, and the king has sequestered himself in his chambers. And did not the king bar you from one of his feasts?"

"A small thing, lieutenant." Iyar pushed a fistful of shekels toward the soldier.

The lieutenant ignored the gesture, instead choosing to pull on his wiry beard. "No, it wasn't. You shamed the man and his house. He ran from you in fear."

"An old memory. The man lives well now, and I hold no fees over him. But please, tell the king that Lord Iyar is here with an important message. I represent my ancestors, not myself."

"All messages are important, as is every noble lineage," the lieutenant said. "Nothing is as important as this union and the lineage it begins. You can see him at the public feast with the other nobles. Perhaps the king will overlook your previous rudeness and allow you to speak."

The next morning, Iyar returned to the palace. Another lieutenant stood on duty with a small company. Two of his kitchen slaves brought baskets of bread, fish, and fruit. They placed the baskets at the soldiers' feet.

Iyar nodded to the lieutenant. "Even soldiers need to eat. Sup."

The men ogled the baskets but waited for their lieutenant's command, who tore off a piece of bread and munched on the crust. "From the bakery in the northeast corner of the city. Nothing rivals its taste. Bread for kings, but the poor buy it."

"Peace or war rest in my words for the king," Iyar said.

"Men, you may eat," the lieutenant said.

The soldiers dived into the baskets, gobbling bread and chewing dates.

The lieutenant bit into a second chunk of bread. "Thank you for the food. But Lord Iyar, your message can wait until the king weds."

Iyar placed his right hand on a dagger. "I cannot wait. Heed me, soldier. If you do not, I will seek your mother and father, sister and brother and find out what debts they have and who owns their debts."

The soldier dropped the bread. "Leave before my dagger finds your throat."

After a heavy meal, and late into the night, Iyar buried the tablets beneath the floor of his home. When he was confident he had hidden the tablets, he stumbled to bed because his body bore the exhaustion, disappointment, and confusion erupting within him. He hadn't sold textiles. He hadn't hosted a feast celebrating his return. He had spent his time entertaining the myths of an old man, running from a structure that emerged from the empty air, reading a terrifying account about his ancestors, and begging impudent soldiers to grant an audience with the king who hated him. How Iyar wished Gabar, and his three odd companions, had never found his desert tent.

Finally, the merchant rested. He dreamed of Yissak. They sat together at sunset.

"I am a man of profit, not sacred purpose, Father. Give this task to Abigail. The tablets are too much for me to bear. I pity what happened to the first Iyar and his son, but I do not want to lose my money. I do not want to appear foolish, and I certainly do not want to die for my sins. Or the sins of my ancestors."

Yissak looped an arm around Iyar's shoulders. "We cannot always choose our moments to be purposeful men and women. But when those moments arrive, always choose purpose. Our inheritance lies in guarding the tablets."

"Why did you not tell me when you were alive?"

Yissak gripped Iyar's shoulders. "Choose purpose. Remember what I told you?"

"Yes, yes, yes. But I do not want to answer. I choose not to answer to anyone."

The sunset ended, and with its fading, Yissak vanished. The dream was over.

The slave girl who hunched her shoulders when she walked served Iyar broth and vegetables for his evening meal. She placed the food on the table, her thick brown hair shrouding every facial expression, her pale, thin fingers trembling.

When Iyar shooed her away, she tightened the downward curl of her shoulders and dashed from the room. Iyar noted he would demand Levi select more pleasing slaves, at least someone with more personality than river weeds.

When Iyar rose the next morning, he felt lightheaded and weak, but he needed to reach Abigail. He assumed she would attend the king's wedding, but he couldn't be certain.

Abigail had settled years ago in Nifla, antagonizing Iyar with her distance. She also offended him by prattling about his imported furniture and rugs, the etched gold lamps, and the large feasts.

Resentment within him deepened, especially after last year, when their brother Eli passed to the realm of their fathers and mothers. Sister and brother said little as they stood at Eli's tomb. When she visited the city, she went to his children's homes and refused to stay with him.

And yet he missed her. Abigail not only made him laugh, but she was also the only person who reminded him of their father's joy, strength, and wisdom. If she responded to his message, he could enlist her help. Trying to reach the king on his own had failed. If she came to his home, maybe Iyar would share his dream about their father. Maybe.

He rubbed his forehead and stomach. Had the plate of vegetables and broth from last night satisfied him? Or had it sickened him? Levi probably added too much salt and basil leaves.

The dizziness increased. The writing stylus weighed on his fingers like heavy rocks. "Naphtali!"

The boy scurried to him. "My lord? Why is your face ashen?"

"I know not. Finish my message for me."

"Of course." Naphtali took the tablet from him.

"To Abigail, the dear."

Iyar sighed. "No, do not say that. She is not dear to me. I am fond."

"Yes, my lord."

"Of even my children, I am only fond. Where are they? Have they visited my house?"

"Jabin sent word that they will arrive before the wedding feast, my lord."

"They intend to flaunt before their friends with my trinkets. Yes, I am only fond. Only you are dear to me, Naphtali."

"I am your slave. Expendable when you choose. I cannot be dear."

"I deserve that."

Iyar wiped perspiration from his face. "I want you to know where the tablets are, Naphtali. I buried them beneath this house. They are a wedding gift for King Shammah. You must direct my sister to them."

"Yes, my lord. But aren't you attending the wedding? This sickness will ease by then. You probably overate. It could be the salt too. When Cook Levi hurries, he adds too much."

"Perhaps. You will need the fastest messenger you can find. You know where the money sack is. Use it as you need. I trust you. Now let us start again. 'To Abigail. Of whom I am fond. My sister. I have learned by a surprising circumstance about our family history.'"

Naphtali wrote, and Iyar nodded before continuing. "'Abigail, it is of the utmost importance. Of course, you plan to witness King Shammah's wedding. He is a servant of Aleph, as are you. He is the first king to claim allegiance to the Existing One. Is that not true? Meet me in the City of Kings at our family home before the ceremony.'"

Iyar paused. "Perhaps that sounds demanding?"

"I will write: 'Please honor me by joining me in the City of Kings,'" Naphtali said.

He scribbled the symbols on the tablet in neat but boyish script before holding up the tablet for Iyar to read.

"Very good." Iyar nodded again before his shoulders sagged.

Naphtali put down the tablet and searched for peppermint oil in a cabinet. He finger-tipped a few drops beneath Iyar's nose. The merchant didn't revive, but slumped in his chair, head on his chest.

That night, Naphtali went to Iyar's chambers before sleeping himself. When Naphtali entered, Iyar nearly fell from his couch, and the slave ran to catch him.

"I'll summon the physician," Naphtali said.

Iyar heaved with frustration. "He is a sorcerer without spells. An herb priest without powers. Get me broth. Hot. Then retrieve the tablets. Abigail should arrive in time."

"I've heard no word from her."

"She will come. Get the tablets."

After making Iyar broth, Naphtali found the spot in the home's lower level where Iyar hid the tablets. Naphtali's fingers crawled through the dirt. *Where were the tablets? Had he missed the location Iyar mentioned? No.* Beneath a mound of earth, he found a piece of cloth, but without its unearthly sheen. Thieves had stolen the rest when robbing the tablets.

Naphtali smoothed the earthen floor and sat on his haunches. Who had seen his master hide the tablets? Who else would know they meant something?

He returned to his master's chambers, frowning and twisting the lock of hair that fell on his narrow forehead.

"Where are they?" Iyar said from his bed.

"A thief lurks in your house."

"No one saw me. I took care. How can the tablets be missing?"

Naphtali tried to still his master's flailing by stretching his arms across his master. Iyar kept tossing, and Naphtali didn't know how long he could hold him down. He wrinkled his nose at the heat and sourness rising from his master's unwashed chest.

A howl barreled through Iyar and Naphtali felt it. "It cannot be. It cannot be."

Naphtali held on. "Only one group benefits, my lord. See this with knowledge. Remember how you taught me to select merchandise carefully? Avoid the eager sellers whose shops look about to crumble. Pay attention to those who show confidence in their work, whose wares are well-made."

Iyar brought his body to rest. "What do you mean by benefits? Speak clearly, boy. I am sick in the stomach, not in the ears."

"Livnath. The priests of the moon goddess may have stolen the tablets."

Naphtali let Iyar go and started pacing. "How, I do not know. Maybe she wants to keep Seth from knowing about the City of the Great King."

"Of course, of course. That is why I rushed to see the palace. Alas, I could not see the king. Money and delicacies from my table did not assuage those idiot lieutenants. But I failed. I have never lost a caravan. But I lost them. I lost the tablets of my ancestors."

CHAPTER FIVE

BURNING HANDS

Jabin tapped hard on Iyar's chamber door. Barak, standing next to him, pulled on a splinter in his thumb. A splinter gained more attention than the fact that they rarely visited their father, that he was the stranger who reared them in luxury, who carried them with him on his caravans until they reached puberty, and the man who supported them in a loose, remote way when they created their shops within the mercantile classes.

Jabin sold properties, and Barak worked for Jabin when he wasn't calling in debts from his wealthy friends. Their sister, Keziah, invested in merchandise that interested her like the merchant who sold blocks of lapis lazuli from the northern kingdoms. She succeeded at it, although she conceded that her most notable feat would be to marry a wealthy noble like her father. Money without marriage wouldn't carry her far in the City of Kings.

"It is my right hand. Every time I move, I feel it," Barak said.

Jabin groaned and knocked harder on his father's door.

"By the dust of the city, enter and stop making that noise," Iyar said.

The room reeked of sweat when the young men stepped inside. Iyar perched on his stool near a balcony overlooking the City of Kings, wearing a scowl that matched the mood of an inconsolable toddler instructed to stay indoors.

Iyar acknowledged his sons with a brief lift of his hand. "I expect you to represent my house before the throne. Be gracious, for once."

Jabin ignored the barb. "Father, are you sure you don't want us to call the physician? All we have heard is that you contracted a stomach sickness, but you refused help."

"The physician owes me money and speaks omens of death. I will rely on my herbs. I am relying on you to represent my house."

Barak refused to conceal a smirk. "Poppies grow in abundance in your gardens. Its juice could soothe your pain."

"You covet the profits from harvesting them," Iyar said.

Jabin groaned. His father was a constant affliction. "Is there a message you wish me to forward to the king? Perhaps an apology to accompany the wedding gift?"

"No message will come from either of you," Iyar said. "All I ask is that the both of you, along with your sister, attend the wedding and that the king sees you. Is that understood? I will send along the gift through Naphtali."

Barak let go of his thumb. "Send the wedding gift through that unwashed creature? Father, are you really intent on irritating King Shammah?"

"You suckle on how you look to people," Iyar said. "Have you not got your fill of compliments and accolades? How does your dress speak to your character? All it says is that you are wealthy, a man with an enviable inheritance. Where is Keziah?"

Barak frowned, confused. He let his bottom lip fall. Then his face brightened when he decided he didn't care what Iyar said.

"Keziah is with the robe makers," Barak said. "The textiles you sent made her deliciously happy."

"Good. Maybe she'll make me happy and attract a husband. In fact, if the king's wedding leads to nuptials for all three of you, I will rejoice."

Jabin attempted to imagine his father rejoicing over them, but he couldn't. Thankfully, Iyar faced the balcony and didn't catch Jabin's frown. As the eldest, Jabin saw his father swing from kindness to apathy, emotional lurches that harassed the boy Jabin and scarred the man.

"The sword you brought me from Edrei was exquisite," Barak said. "I will wear it to the wedding."

"Good. And your gift, Jabin?"

"The jeweled dagger was the perfect choice."

"Good, good. Now, go away. The sun sets."

They left. Jabin and his brother were aware of their father's peculiar habit during sunsets. They never minded the ritual because their grandfather Yissak, like his ancestors, had left the family extremely wealthy, although their father often complained that Yissak was frugal to a fault, that he reared the family in the poorer section of the City of Kings, and donated too many shekels to the poor.

But the fact remained that Yissak was not only kind but shrewd. He negotiated the best prices and won the respect of the merchants, and those who remembered him recalled his name with fondness.

Maybe, Jabin mused, his father's meditations about Yissak would make him kinder toward them. He shook his head and laughed, which caused Barak to stop in the hallway and touch Jabin's arm.

"Tell me the source of your mirth," Barak said.

"For a moment," Jabin said, "I thought our father could become a sweeter man and share his knowledge of commerce with us."

"Why anoint yourself with false hopes? Of the three of us, you have endured his selfishness the most."

"Forget the cage in which our father has held us captive? Never."

Naphtali squatted at the threshold of the kitchen where his sister Hulda worked. She shucked peas, toted baskets, and peeled onions until he didn't know whether she ached from the basket loads or the onions.

The cook never appreciated Hulda's skills and never let her do more. It was always peas, onions, and baskets of food. Today, Naphtali promised to walk with her through the bazaar and buy her cloth for a new tunic. Hulda adored clothes even when they were thinning with wear. If she envied the nobles anything, she longed to drape herself with the new garments they flaunted.

Hulda plopped next to him on the threshold with a scented wave of onions. "Dreaming about what, brother? The cook doesn't need me for the afternoon."

"No dreams. Pure hopes. Are you ready?"

They sprinted to the bazaar down the skinny streets they knew so well. Naphtali spotted the corner where they had begged for food for two days. Under a mangled tree that still stood, they slept when moonlight swept the city.

Naphtali stopped at a scribe's booth. He was selling clay tablets, and a hot kiln behind him was ready to bake in the message.

"A message for your true love, boy?" asked the scribe. The waxen-faced-merchant wore a purple turban that needed adjusting on his head, and his lips disappeared within the puffy hairs of his beard when he spoke.

"No," Naphtali said. "Are you really a scribe?"

"I'm selling tablets, aren't I?"

Naphtali shrugged, unconvinced. The man probably never lifted a stylus. Naphtali kept walking toward Hulda, who caressed cloth in a nearby booth.

"Many of the scribes aren't as literate as they pretend to be," she said. Hulda never raised her eyes while she stroked the fabric.

Naphtali sighed. Hulda missed nothing. "His lack of literary acumen doesn't concern me. He behaves like a clever thief. The tablets he sells more than likely he stole."

"By the sky and Earth," Hulda said. "Only last night I overheard my master tell the cook about strange tablets no one should handle. Master placed them in his chamber. They burned at his touch."

"Burned?"

Hulda trotted to the next booth. "Master's palms blistered red as pomegranates. Cook wrapped his hands three times."

Naphtali's voice sneaked from his lips in a squeak. "Where did your master get the tablets?"

"If I didn't know that you were my little brother, I would think you were a chick." Hulda giggled. "When will the man in you overcome the voice of a boy? What was I saying? Yes. I don't know where the tablets came from. They're in his chambers. Cook had them placed on planks so that no one could touch them. The high priest plans to view them. Why is that? Friends also visited master the other night. Lots of guffawing about Livnath. And all I wanted to know is why hasn't Livnath made my master richer so I can stop peeling his onions?"

A horse cart wobbled near her, and Naphtali swung Hulda away from it within moments. "Be careful, Sister."

"Thank you, little Brother," Hulda said. "Such strength. Maybe you're not a boy anymore."

Balled in the bed like a street cat, Hulda's master slept without noise. The dying light of an oil lamp burned. Scattered cups on the floor meant wine had pushed the man into a sound sleep, enabling Naphtali to move around the room undetected.

Naphtali reached the far side of the room. He combed the wall shelves with his fingers. He grunted in the semi-darkness and feared stumbling over furniture or one of the plump cats he often saw parading in the kitchen. After foraging for food every night in the city streets and trying to avoid feral cats, Hulda and Naphtali despised the creatures.

Naphtali hit a stool with his big toe. Naphtali threw his fingers between his lips. A silent howl ran through his chest. What was the stool made of? Rocks? He waited for the aching to subside before continuing to search the shelf. His fingers danced across linen. Could this be the tablets? He kept touching the tablets, trying to remember how the wrapped tablets felt in Iyar's tent. He couldn't tell.

"By the sky and Earth." His voice imitated Hulda's. Naphtali frowned. Why was he speaking aloud? Did he want to be gutted in a noble's bedroom?

Naphtali continued searching the shelf. In the darkness appeared a gold, unnatural light. Behind it, wrapped in linen, then partially covered in the ripped, but glimmering fabric, lay the tablets Gabar had given his master. Naphtali cocked his head. *The fabric revealed its unnatural light at will. Remember to think about that later,* he thought.

Naphtali grabbed the tablets. He retraced his steps to the door and his toes felt warm fur. The cat shrieked. Naphtali's stomach twisted. He leaped through a window near Hulda's master's bed, slid down the wall and awning.

When his feet hit the ground, Naphtali groaned because his toe throbbed again. He ignored the ache and raced to Iyar's home. Naphtali didn't hear voices shouting after him, and he never looked back to listen.

A diminutive figure lay in a heap on the sailing vessel when Ezer, the high priest, arrived. Before he stepped on the shoreline, dank odors wafted from the vessel with its small sail. Ezer didn't know whether the smell emanated from the vessel or the figure that unraveled its body when Ezer approached.

Their escort appeared to be mortal. But the stringy hair and the webbed hand the figure extended confirmed that this creature was their escort into the Time Sea.

Ezer nodded and gestured to the short man with him. "Resist speaking, Qatsar."

They seated themselves in the vessel, where small barbels twisted in pools of water on the floor. A few bones lay nearby, and Ezer guessed their escort had chewed the barbel raw.

"Do not address it," Ezer said to Qatsar, who looked offended by the filthy water pooling around them.

The escort dipped an oar into the foamy water. The vessel moved from the shore until the lamp lights of Yaphah appeared far away.

After about an hour, the escort threw off his cloak, and his full, scaly body appeared. The escort was both fish and man. Gills and fins fluttered when he began rowing with speed. The sea pulled back, a bowing servant parting to make room. An unseen grip drew the vessel into a vertical tunnel.

Ezer and Qatsar clung to the vessel as it spun through the tunnel. The vessel landed on a shoreline illuminated by a pale light. Both Ezer and his companion gulped for breath.

"Drink this," the escort said. He pulled two vials from his smelly cloak. "It will keep you alive in our territory."

Frowning, the men sipped the drink. The liquid stung, but their labored breathing eased.

When they disembarked, two tall soldiers, also with pale, stringy hair and carrying fish hooks and spears, escorted them from the shore through a series of caves, each different from the other, varying in light and texture. They stopped at a large cave that opened to a pond of water where sea horses fought each other in the waters.

"What news do you have for me?" Zalmon asked them, his keen gaze taking in their discomfort and anxiety. "I'll not snare you with a hook. Maybe later. If the sea horses tire and become famished."

The first time Ezer met Zalmon, the same horror he felt now hung on his limbs like wet, muscled arms.

Zalmon sat on his golden, algae-covered throne, and clinging beside him was Mahalath, Shammah's first bride, once a thoughtful beauty who had become a sycophant, appearing unwashed and slightly green.

"We succeeded," Ezer said. "Partially."

"Explain."

"Qatsar retrieved the vial from Aleph's priest."

The short Qatsar, his flattened ears aflame in a blush, scurried before Zalmon with a quick bow. Zalmon spoke before the man could speak.

"What do you have for me?" Zalmon's harsh tone gurgled from him.

Mahalath giggled. Bellows from the sea king failed to send Mahalath running to a corner, and Zalmon swelled his chest because of it, delighted by her ease in his presence.

The man pulled a sealed jar from his robes and handed it to Zalmon. "A wedding gift from the Zuzim, my lord. They told me where and how to retrieve it."

Zalmon tossed the sealed jar between his webbed hands. "The secret of Aleph that defeated the Mikana is now among the Water People."

"How will you use it, my lord?" Mahalath ran her fingers over her face and hair.

"A weapon stolen becomes a weapon lost." Zalmon broke the seal and poured out the amber liquid, which scorched the sand as it fell.

"Ruined sand," the man said.

"A small cost," Mahalath said.

When the jar was empty, Zalmon crushed the jar with his fingers. "Aleph hides its use. We cannot extract them. But we can keep them from being used."

"A weapon lost," Mahalath said.

"What else?" Zalmon said to Ezer.

"We lost the tablets of Iyar. One of our allies hid them for us, but someone stole them from him. We have not found the thief, but we have our suspicions."

"What else?"

"We poisoned Iyar, hoping that would slow him from studying the tablets and taking them to Shammah. So far, it has worked. The sickness remains."

"Very good. Disrupt the wedding."

Ezer couldn't help himself. He cut a look at Mahalath, wondering how news of Shammah's upcoming nuptials affected her, but she lolled at Zalmon's side, seaweed tangling her legs and ankles.

"May all eyes fix on Livnath. No one else," Zalmon continued.

Ezer straightened his shoulders, although he longed to rub his stomach because of a growing desire to retch. "We have made arrangements."

"Arrangements. Do you imagine yourself reclining with the nobles at a feast under the stars and discussing this? What I demand may require crawling in the dust, sliding through the dank, and living with the maggots. I demand subjugation, lest my fishhook snatch the meat from your bones for my sea horses to chew."

Every move Dahv took, Princess Naamah followed, then every evening, she rehearsed what she saw. She lay on her bed, thinking about his mannerisms and how he parried with her father, Zalmon, and the priests of Livnath, Qayin and Haran, about ancient histories and the rights of the throne. Thinking about Dahv intoxicated her.

The attraction she felt didn't spring solely from the fact that he was royalty; Dahv was handsome, a comic who made her giggle when he wasn't melancholy for daylight and Earth. Dahv drew her to him, like water coating rock, because he was shrewd.

As the ousted king of Seth, he had accepted his lot and found a place under her father's protection. She felt the insistent resilience beneath his words that echoed the belief that his watery prison wouldn't hold him forever. His longing for freedom drove Naamah's longing for him.

One memory she cherished was catching Dahv sitting alone and writing on a tablet. She was collecting flora sprouting near the ponds. Seeing him had caused her heart to race with anxiety, but the desire to hear his voice overrode her fears.

"May I join you?" She hid her trembling hands beneath the basket of flora.

"Of course, Lady Naamah." He made space on the large rock where he sat, and she placed her basket between them.

"Your flowers are beautiful," Dahv said. "It is beyond my understanding that flowers grow here without sunlight."

Naamah blushed as his soft tone washed over her. "They're not real flowers, so everyone tells me. They spring from the waters, not the Earth."

"You have not traveled above the waters?"

She rubbed her hands together and then twisted the braid that fell from her ear to waist. "I have dreamed of it. "

"Dreaming without walking the Earth. You are beneath the sea, not dead."

"Father fears me traveling there to Seth and your kingdom."

"What causes his fear? He is no coward. Neither are you, I would wager, though your demeanor is gentle."

"Something happens to us when we are above. No one gives me a straightforward answer, and I have found nothing that explains it. The histories tell me nothing."

Naamah touched the tablet in Dahv's hands. "What were you reading, my lord? Are you learning about my people?"

"Actually, tablets about the wars of the Water People. The acumen of your ancestors' military makes me rethink my battle training."

"I have read some of those stories. The battle with the sea horses is my favorite. Our warriors used sea foam ropes to subdue them."

"Learning about weaponry brought you delight? Forgive me for underestimating your interest. I figured you as the reclining type."

Naamah had hung her head, blushing again.

"Have I offended you? I did not mean to." He bent toward her, searching her face.

"No, my lord," she had said with a gulp, reaching for her basket. "You did not offend me. You never do. I must go."

Naamah groaned at the memory and sat up in her bed. Reliving that interlude made her flush. She never knew what to say to Dahv; there was so much she wanted him to know, especially about her.

On the day of King Shammah's wedding, Jabin and Barak lounged in their father's courtyard. They waited for their sister, Keziah, to join them in the procession to the palace. Keziah was always late, and no amount of preparation changed that fact. Jabin thought she took pleasure in ignoring the wishes of others. Her desires enslaved everyone and aroused competition among her suitors while irritating her brothers.

"She will be tardy for her death," Barak said. He chewed a date, then spat it out. "Dry. Old. Take it away."

Head bowed and mumbling, a nearby slave removed the tray of dates and scurried from the room. Barak relished frightening slaves, Jabin thought. He also delighted in tormenting animals with decayed food to see whether they recovered or died.

"Discernment seeps from my father's thoughts. He can't calculate the way he once did," Barak said.

His frown mirrored someone stepping over a pile of dung, Jabin thought. His face, so much like their father's, along with his thick black hair, couldn't hide the youthful impatience.

"He does not notice that his slaves rebel," Barak said. "He loses money with their presence."

Jabin stared at his younger brother with an expression that would appear as pity. But Jabin felt no such thing. Spoiled and petulant, Barak's presence was more aggravating than the desert sun without a tent.

"Father sees," Jabin said. He leaned his shoulder on a pillar, his hands behind him, and observed Barack with disinterest. "Rebellion never persists without him as witness."

"You chastise me, Brother?" Barak reached for a pear.

"Would you feel the wound?"

Jabin turned his attention to his sister, who joined them, paying little attention to the slaves adjusting the belt at her waist and the dark-blue ribbons on her shoulder. Her blue-black hair glistened, and her eager expression washed over her brothers, demanding masculine approval.

Jabin refused. He lifted himself from the pillar. "The cart waits outside."

"Sister, you irritated our brother." Barak wiped his mouth. "You made him wait. Your suitors will pay more attention to you than the king's desert bride. You are indeed lovely today."

"I have never seen the queen," said Keziah at last. She shooed the slaves away. "The gossips say she has hands as large as a farmer's."

"And hair as wiry as desert plants," chimed in Barak.

"Myths from a bored, useless, noble class and their equally purposeless slaves," Jabin said. "When will it cease?"

"You are one of that class," Barak said. "And a firstborn son. You cannot conceal your birth, Brother. But why care about this roughly hewn queen speckled with dust? She gained a throne as soon as the king chose her as his wife. My heart doesn't dance with anticipation. The royal nuptials are simply an opportunity for me to study the delectable maidens who long for an audience with me, a rich aristocrat. King Shammah chose his love. I intend to choose mine. Only two days ago, father said that's what he wanted. Spouses to multiply the house of Iyar."

Keziah searched the room. "Is Father coming with us?"

"No," said Jabin. "He takes to his bed, still."

"He will not see my garments. I will show him later," Keziah said with mock sadness.

"Did you see him today, Brother?" Barak nibbled on a piece of salted meat.

"Naphtali informed me."

"The rodent of the lower classes," Barak said. "Father trots him around like a pet, and with very little effort, Naphtali repels the masses."

"Ah, but an incredibly smart pet," Jabin said.

"Why do you say that? You are defending him," said Keziah. "I agree with Barak. He repulses me. Father needs me to assign slaves for him."

Barak studied Jabin's face, which he shuttered like a window before a storm. "He knows something, Keziah. But will he tell us?"

Keziah lifted a hand, waiting for her oldest brother to grasp it. "Perhaps. Jabin, you may escort me out."

Jabin kept his hands linked behind him, grinned, and offered a swift bow. "Barak is far more skilled at escorting. I will follow."

"Keep watch on my children and for an opportunity to see the king," Iyar said to Naphtali from his bed. "You must tell the king about the tablets. Abigail must be with you. Have you seen my sister?"

Naphtali lifted a lock that kept falling to his forehead. "The slaves say she's going directly to the nuptials today."

"Did she visit my house?"

"The slaves said she asked about you before the birds sang. After that, she left."

"Another slight. Find Abigail in the crowd and say that I demand to see her. You will recognize her by height. Tall, with pale skin and ruby hair that glows with the sun. She will wear gold robes. It is her favorite color for events like these. When you reach her, tell her that my message is about our ancestors. Then we will take the tablets together to the king."

"If she refuses?"

"She must not ignore you. She cannot."

"Yes, my lord."

Iyar breathed hard and turned pale. "You gave the Midvar wine in its ornamental jar for the king as my wedding gift, correct?"

"Three slaves delivered the wine jar to the palace yesterday," Naphtali said.

"The king had better savor each drop," Iyar said. "There is no more of it."

Iyar pulled himself up in the bed, and Naphtali heard the trembling in his master's voice. "When you recovered the tablets, did you place them in the cabinet as I instructed you?"

A cabinet in an unused room where spiders captured every corner wasn't a safe place for tablets that would change the destiny of the Seth.

Iyar was too sick to understand that he couldn't protect the tablets in his house. Someone among them was a thief. It was Naphtali's burden to guard them.

"Master," Naphtali said. "I secured them."

Iyar lay back on the bed. "Tell me again. How did you discover the tablets? I must apprehend the thief."

Naphtali hadn't told him. Even among his master's friends, there was betrayal. For now, at least, it was better Iyar didn't know.

CHAPTER SIX

THE APPRENTICE

Queen Tamiym's caravan from Chaniya waited outside the city gates, and the drums acknowledged her arrival. A marching rhythm emerged from the drums, like warriors thudding earth or fists pounding hundreds of tables.

Naphtali's heart beat faster as he stepped over the street pebbles, the mounds of horse dung, the flowing garments of the noblewomen, and the pesky ravens who pecked at bits of food littering patches of dirt.

Naphtali felt carried by the drums. Perhaps he felt that way because he hadn't obeyed Iyar's instructions explicitly. He didn't leave the tablets in the cabinet Iyar specified. Naphtali bound them to his slim body beneath layers of garments, making him appear stockier.

Bringing the tablets as King Shammah's wedding gift was the best thing to do. King Shammah needed the tablets. The palace didn't require the Midvar wine Iyar instructed Naphtali to give. Shammah needed the truth.

The drumbeats pounded in his ears. Naphtali squeezed between two nobles to glimpse the queen's caravan. Sapphire and silver banners adorned the cart, accompanied by horses and camels. Gold-colored cloth covered the queen's cart, concealing the queen, as the crowds shouted accolades. She slipped out a slender hand in response but didn't show her face.

Naphtali scanned the crowds, searching for his master's sister among the clusters of nobles. No one fit her description. He navigated his way along the route the queen's caravan was taking toward a platform in the Gardens of Destiny next to the palace.

There, the king waited for her. Unlike the savior-kings of the past who followed Livnath, Shammah held his nuptials in the open and not at Livnath's temple.

Naphtali pressed his way to the edges of the Gardens of Destiny, ambling behind slaves carrying platters until he found a platter to tote inside where another group of aristocrats waited, pompous and impatient. If his master's sister weren't here, Naphtali didn't know how he would deliver the tablets to the king.

Suddenly, he also imagined a wrathful Gabar slicing him from shoulder to waist with his sword because he failed. Shaken by the thought, he put down the platter to avoid dropping it, then mingled with the slaves as he patted his chest, reassuring himself the tablets remained strapped to his ribs. Being unable to find Abigail heightened his desire to reach Shammah with the tablets himself.

The crowd made room for the king as he approached the platform in robes of sapphire-blue and white, the diadem of Seth glistening over his thick braids. Giddy with joy, the king ascended the platform steps two at a time, his sandals clapping on the stone.

When the king reached the top, he smiled at the man Naphtali assumed would perform the nuptials, then turned toward an approaching caravan. Shammah brushed his lips as if to hide his growing smile. He paced. He threw back his head and laughed. The priest nudged him to be still.

Naphtali, agitated like the king, elbowed a few slaves so he could watch more closely.

The queen's caravan was moments away. Shammah descended the steps in a trot to meet his bride once she stepped from her cart.

Naphtali stood within a handbreadth of the cart and Shammah. The time had come. Wiggling between several matrons, the boy reached out to the king, who was now in front of the cart, and he prepared to open his tunic and thrust the tablets to the king.

But someone yanked Naphtali by his neck, like jarring him from a dream, and dragged him back into the crowd.

Naphtali heard a woman's voice, husky and stern. "Naphtali, I think you're searching for me."

Towering above him was Abigail, dressed in embroidered gold robes as his master predicted.

"Now is not the time."

With an arm curved around his shoulders, Abigail guided him to a quiet corner, while still in view of the wedding procession. "We can watch everything from here," she said.

Shammah flung back the cart's veil, lifted Tamiym in his arms, and carried her to the platform, her face still covered. Tamiym caressed his cheek as he smiled down at her.

Once at the top of the platform, Shammah helped Tamiym stand with a gentle swoop.

King Shammah's brazenness annoyed Naphtali, whom Iyar disciplined in protocol. Everything about the marriage ceremony was awry. "The king behaves oddly. The queen must ascend toward him, the savior king."

Abigail's arm tightened around Naphtali's shoulders, a gesture both comforting and entrapping. "A guardian of protocol? You leap over boundaries as well, Naphtali."

"How do you know anything?" Resentment grew within him. In response, Abigail held him tighter.

"I was on a mission," he stammered. "Gabar gave my master and me the tablets. I mean, gave my master. Gabar gave my master the tablets. Thieves stole them from deep in my master's home's floor, where he thought they would be safe. Then I found the thief, with the help of my sister Hulda, and stole them back."

"But you wanted to give them to the king," Abigail said. "Alone."

Naphtali writhed beneath Abigail's arm, trapped like a flea, but this only made her touch harder. When he relaxed, she loosened her grip.

"You wanted to fulfill destiny on your own."

"How do you know this?"

"Aleph."

"A busy deity doesn't care for the welfare of slaves. But my master is sick, Lady Abigail. Fever turns his mind. Or some demon from the underworld. He's not been right since we left the desert. He wanted me to find you, but you found me first. I could blame this on you. You refused to meet with my master."

"Have you read the tablets?"

"Only what my master and I read together in the desert. I know it involves your family history and Seth's origins."

"You read nothing else?"

"I sought to protect the tablets and get them to King Shammah."

"Some protocols you understand."

Abigail diverted her scorching stare to the platform and the man placing his hands on the shoulders of the king and queen.

"Is that man a priest?"

Abigail gave a smile wide as a river. "Yes. Chazon, priest of Aleph."

The priest's words were faint from where Naphtali and Abigail stood: "May Aleph bless . . . keep . . . your union . . . the kingdom . . ."

"May it be so." Abigail's loud voice joined others.

Naphtali looked up at her. "Do you believe in their love?"

"I do."

"My master doubts it. He views the queen as a farm girl hungry for an elevated station. Few find love, he says."

"Someone he loved hurt him, you know."

"Master?"

"Someone withheld love from my brother Iyar, in the unkindest of ways." Abigail broke the sternness in her voice as Shammah lifted the veil from Tamiym's face.

Tamiym's beauty and the love dancing between the queen and king stunned Naphtali. He now understood why Shammah appeared smitten. Tamiym wasn't pasty in appearance from creams or wide-eyed from kohl; her skin glowed bronze and her deep-brown gaze hugged Shammah as he stood before her.

When she raised a hand to cut the king's jaw, Naphtali felt his heart stir. Tamiym wore lasting beauty like a sheen from the sun, the kind no wrinkle of age could defile.

"One day, you will know love like this, Naphtali," Abigail said.

Abigail recognized the longing within him. He looked down and shuffled his feet. "You have sight?"

"Aleph gives visions. He showed me you."

"Will you tell my master what I've done? He will beat me. I may lose my rank. By the pigs and rats, I don't want to build mud houses or carry reeds and water."

"I will not tell him."

"Why are you showing me kindness? You don't know me."

"Because, one day, you will keep secrets of mine."

Abigail chose a seat at a far table against a wall. No one sat near them, but the king and queen were in clear view, bobbing among the guests, always within a touch of each other.

Stuffy air filled the courtyard, but Shammah and Tamiym seemed unbothered by the warmth.

Although her face beamed with happiness, Abigail seemed content not to greet them. She insisted Naphtali sit on a stool near her and that he prepared a full plate. Naphtali felt restrained but grateful for the food and the leisure to observe others without serving them.

As he chomped a chunk of lamb between his lips, Abigail leaned toward him while keeping Shammah and Tamiym in view.

"It is no accident that the desert horsemen brought the tablets to my brother in the desert."

Naphtali almost choked. Did nothing pass this woman unseen?

"*Malakim* came to you in the desert," Abigail said. "Aleph determined now is time to reveal the truth about the sacred founding."

"What's *malakim*?"

"The four men you met are *malakim*. Messengers from Aleph. They roam our winds."

"They mentioned winds."

"Did they?" Abigail tore a piece of bread.

"They also blew winds on us. Like a whirlwind. They seemed to unleash the skies."

His reply didn't ruffle Abigail as Naphtali intended.

"A foretaste of the turbulence to come. Learn to gird yourself from fear, Naphtali. The whirlwind of Aleph will dismantle false kingdoms, but first there will be war. Shammah must not see the tablets until the war begins."

"Wouldn't the tablets help him now? And isn't that what Gabar instructed my master to do?"

Abigail's eyes narrowed. "Both you and my brother, Iyar, presumed. Aleph gave the tablets as weapons of knowledge. Warriors wield swords and spears for a destined time. Should they fight too early, they battle phantoms. When the enemy bursts through the gates, they war unprepared. If warriors wait too long, fear saps their strength. The enemy conquers because they hesitated.

"After the Great Deluge, the elders gave the tablets to the house of Iyar. Aleph appointed our house to guard them."

Naphtali felt the acrid taste of rebellion rising within him. "People could die. My parents died when the Mikana fought King Shammah. I understand the terrors war brings. It left my sister and me orphans, then slaves."

"A burning heart receives satisfaction if it waits for the doors of refuge to open. Can you trust this?"

Naphtali felt Abigail's succinct question dredge up every disappointment and root of anger. "I will try." He paused. "If you tell me your secrets."

She erupted with loud laughter, throwing back her long, lean neck. A few of the nobles eyed them. A few men also noticed Abigail's wind-tossed beauty.

"Aleph buried the tablets in this land before an earthly kingdom or king existed. They carry the dimensions of an unseen city, glorious in beauty, the throne of the Existing One, the Great King. Livnath seduced the second Iyar, only a boy like you, to give her the tablets, which were in the care of his father, one of the first elders of Seth. With the tablets, Livnath claimed to be Seth's patroness and claimed authority for it in the heavens and on the Earth. When you hear someone speak about the sacred founding, they are referring to that time in Seth's history. Nothing was sacred. It was an unholy uprising intended to stop and defame the plans of Aleph."

Naphtali put down his lamb and then his entire plate. "I thought this deity reigned on that mountain near Yaphah, sometimes with a gloomy facade of storms and lightning. How can Aleph be here and there? Does Aleph have two homes?"

"How can Aleph not be? Would you consign less power to Aleph when Livnath soars as the moon, as a crone, and as a young woman? Aleph is far more powerful. Alas, Livnath has seduced Seth into ignorance with her myths."

"One more question. When did Aleph retrieve the tablets from Livnath?"

She gave him a grim smile. "A mystery shadows that answer. I can give you my speculation."

Naphtali pulled on a lock of hair. "Even that is better than silence."

"Sometimes silence protects us. Aleph decided the season of captivity was over."

"And where did goddess hide the tablets?"

"Of that, I am more certain. She left them in the care of the Water People. The two tablets stood suspended beneath the waters for generations. The Water People couldn't touch them or read what they said because they burned at the touch. They only knew that the tablets gave Livnath rights to the City of Kings."

"Like Hulda's master." Naphtali shuddered when he remembered how he slipped from his sister's master. If the man had discovered Naphtali, he would have assigned him to a perpetual stack of onions. Or killed him.

"But what mystifies me is the tablets didn't injure me. Why is that? And there are three tablets, not two. What is the significance of the third?"

Abigail either didn't hear Naphtali or ignored the question. She stood up, her back straight, and walked toward the royal table where the king and queen reclined on a large platform.

"Now we will meet the king and queen," she said over her shoulder. "Say nothing of this, young man. You now serve with me, not my brother. After the wedding feast, you return to my home in Nifla, and you will not be a slave."

Naphtali trailed behind her, trying to comprehend what was happening. Freedom came at a word in a sudden circumstance.

Abigail turned. "Your thoughts feel like droplets falling behind me. In a few words, your circumstances changed, and it overwhelms you, does it not?"

Warm tears slid along his cheeks. "Only hours ago, a slave," Naphtali said.

"Aleph sent healing words." Abigail resumed walking.

Naphtali gathered himself and scanned the courtyard, as Iyar trained him to do, counting the tables, the platters, the wine jars, and assessing the crowds, the greedy eaters, the talkative diners, and the guests who slipped food beneath their robes.

This was a skill of slaves, a regimen of their service. Only he did so as a free citizen of Seth. How should he observe his surroundings now that he was free? He had molded himself into slavery and learned to survive as Hulda also had done. Hulda would need to be free too. He prepared himself to say that until he spotted two boys competing for attention before Queen Tamiym.

The boys in the Chaniyan field. They huddled around the queen. How did two bossy boys get that close to the king and queen?

The oldest boy recognized Naphtali, and they exchanged glares. Naphtali focused on the boy so much he collided with Abigail when she jerked to an abrupt stop.

"My lady, my apologies," Naphtali said, stepping back.

"Did you hear that?" Abigail's voice was loud enough for only Naphtali to hear.

Naphtali pivoted his gaze from the glowering boy to Abigail. Voices of people crowding into the feast, along with the clank of platters and cups, faded as he heard the cries of oxen. By the sound of their wails, they were being herded outside the palace. Above the din, Naphtali could also hear priests chanting Livnath's name.

The king and queen held hands, most likely aware only of each other or the nobles pressing for their attention. Naphtali saw that the young boys scampered from the platform to pursue him, and he worried about the ruckus that could cause.

Before he could utter a word to Abigail, she grabbed his arm. "We must go outside."

Wide brown eyes flickered before the oxen died. With each slaughter, the priests poured blood where Livnath's statue once stood. Sethites of all ages once made promises to Livnath from this hump of dirt. On their behalf, Ezer wanted to make a promise to Livnath that the priests would restore her temple. The small shrine on the ridge couldn't replace Livnath's former structure. And by law, Shammah couldn't forbid them from rebuilding on the old temple site. But the priests needed a benefactor to boost their coffers. Otherwise, they could lose their property rights.

Aleph would not deter them from resurrecting her presence. Also, hovering in the high priest's mind, were Zalmon's sardonic references to fishhooks. Haran, Ezer's predecessor, already lived like a lapdog in Zalmon's armpit of seaweed, chewing on barbel until death. The Great War and living beneath the waters silenced Haran into a horrible submission where he never rose to fight for Livnath's cause.

Ezer refused to yield. He cleared his throat and shouted: "Pray so that our patroness hears your prayers. We have not forgotten her."

A small group of Livnath's priests yelled their petitions to the sky. Their cries hadn't been heard in so long that stunned city residents who hadn't gone to Shammah's wedding mingled in the street. A few moments to distract some Sethites from Shammah was worth the cost of killing their best oxen for the sacrifice. This was Livnath's city. Once the priests rebuilt her temple, the people would remember that.

Slaying oxen provided the perfect sacrifice because followers compared Aleph with the great ox, strong and mighty, but Ezer wanted to defile that image on the very day of Shammah's wedding.

The slaughter fed Livnath's pleasure—wood to her celestial fires. The flames of the sacrifice shot upward, blood soaked in the dirt, and the chants rumbled through the ruins.

When Naphtali and Abigail arrived at Livnath's temple site, the fires soared high in the twilight. Blood flowed in thin trails along the temple's foundations. The priests leaped and bore that crazed expression that Naphtali remembered disgusted Iyar.

Naphtali wrinkled his nose. The killings bore a stench. The priests had slaughtered at least thirty oxen from what Naphtali could count as the priests stacked the carcasses and set them ablaze.

Abigail grimaced. "If the odors offend you, how do you think this appears to Aleph? Livnath's slanders the Heavens and defiles the sacred site of Aleph."

"Isn't that the priest who married the king and queen?"

Chazon stood about twenty people ahead of them. He rolled up the sleeves of his tunic and thrust his hands toward the sky, like a babe touching his father's knees.

"He is the priest of Aleph."

"What is he doing? Why leave the nuptials? Why take part in this bloody ritual?"

"Watch. He battles the work of Livnath's priests."

"With his beard or the hairs on his forearms? He doesn't carry a weapon."

"Watch."

Admiration glowed on Abigail's face as she studied Chazon position himself despite the people surrounding him, despite the cries of the oxen or the shouts of the priests.

"Should we help him do whatever you call that posture? The priests have killed many oxen. Many families need oxen. The stench of that waste must revolt your Aleph. I want to retch myself."

"Watch, Naphtali."

Wrapped in forceful concentration, Chazon kept his arms upraised as he danced before an unseen audience. The dance was warlike, pounding the ground like hoofbeats.

As if to accompany him, Abigail lifted her arms and bowed her head. He turned back to Chazon. The priest lay face down in the dirt, drawing the curious. Some of them kicked at him in annoyance. Someone spat because Chazon blocked his way.

Now Abigail was facedown, too, her wedding garments soiled by dirt. Uncertain what to do, Naphtali squatted next to Abigail like the watchmen he'd always seen peering from the city's walls and bearing witness to what was happening.

Naphtali gasped. An apparition appeared from the pools of oxen blood emerged. It was a woman. Naphtali suspected it was Livnath, who gained strength from the cries, the blood, and the carcasses.

At first, she appeared petite, a crone fragile enough to injure with a child's push. Then she shifted into a lovely woman walking barefoot in the muddy mix of dirt and blood. She strolled the ruins, picking up stones and kissing them.

The priests could see her, too, and they shouted as her body defined itself, shimmering with greenish robes.

The vision fragmented. Horror crisscrossed her face.

Naphtali sensed something resisting her and muffling the cries of the priests.

The priests yelled and stomped across the temple site with frenzied twirls. "Livnath. Livnath. Return to your temple!"

As the sun pitched into the western horizon, the four black steeds that Gabar and his desert companions rode galloped toward the temple. The horses appeared as ominous as they did in the desert, and they sounded like armies charging overhead.

The horses blew fire from their mouths. Flames tipped their tails. Precious stones crowned their heads.

The woman howled like a master flogged her mercilessly. But no one stood near her except the horses, who sprayed her with flames.

Livnath's priests kept yelling and slinging blood. Neither the priests nor the crowds gathered around the temple site could see the horses. They only saw the wailing Livnath.

"More blood," the priests cried. Several of them scraped their arms and legs with knives and daggers. "She calls for more."

The horses trampled the makeshift ritual site until the priests, exhausted from shouting and dizzy from their bloodletting, collapsed.

Livnath shrunk back into a small crone, and slithered into the mud. With a moan, she disappeared.

The steeds roared away, smoke encircling them like incense floating upward in the gathering night.

Chazon rose and walked through the crowds, his gait unsteady.

"What were you doing?" The man stepped closer to Chazon, balling his fists.

"He's the priest of Aleph," said a woman. She clung to a battered hand statue of Livnath.

"We should kill him for disturbing the ruins," the man said.

Chazon never turned, but his walk straightened, and the crowd fell back, muttering among themselves.

The priest recognized Abigail as she rose and rushed to assist her.

"Lady Abigail," Chazon said. "I did not know you were here."

The youthful smile on his face grew wider. Abigail smiled back. Naphtali couldn't help staring. Their wide smiles matched each other. Like two rivers.

"Yes," she said. "Petitioning Aleph to protect the City of Kings, alongside you."

"I thought I was alone before the Existing One," Chazon said.

"It was not Livnath's time to return, no matter how desperate she longs for it to be."

Abigail looked at Naphtali. The boy held his hands to his head, confounded by what he witnessed. "Is that what you saw, Naphtali?"

The boy didn't question how Abigail knew what happened to him. She had prayed facedown in the street. "Livnath manifested as a young goddess amid the ruins. I saw her. Then, the horses came." Naphtali winced because his stammering had returned.

"What horses?" Chazon frowned with his eyebrows that appeared as dark tree trunks laid flat across his forehead. Naphtali tried not to giggle about it.

"Four," Naphtali said. "Four black steeds. They appeared to my master and me in the desert. Except this time, only the horses arrived. And, like a broom, they swept away the blood offering in Livnath's temple. They stomped on the site and mashed it as tiny as grains of wheat."

Naphtali imitated the horses' hooves by digging his toes into the dirt.

"The sacrificing stopped because of the horses. One thing I noticed about them. It wasn't there before."

"Go on," said Abigail.

"They wore crowns. With two precious jewels. Jasper. Sardius. I recognize them from my trading with Master."

Abigail and Chazon fell to their knees again.

"What? Did I do something again?"

"The horses had no riders because the Existing One rode them," Abigail said. "Those stones speak of the Great Aleph himself."

"Oh," said Naphtali. Trembling, he looked upward at the darkening sky. "Aleph must want her gone. Really gone. Livnath shrank into this ugly crone and disappeared into the mud. Lady Abigail, I thought Livnath was the most beautiful woman in the world. Livnath's skin appears cracked, like dried earth. I find no beauty in her and would challenge anyone who thought her bewitchment worth captivity."

Chazon drew his brows together. "Are you slave or free, young man?"

"My brother, Iyar, has been his lord," Abigail said.

"Is Iyar with us? After all this time? For many seasons have we waited," Chazon said.

"Because of my brother, the tablets are in Seth." Abigail kept her voice quiet, out of earshot of people who mingled near them. "But because of Naphtali, we guard the tablets."

Naphtali patted his chest. No one could take the tablets away.

Chazon stared at Naphtali without speaking for a long moment. "You are a brave one. May Aleph surround you with power until you reach Nifla safely. At another time, may I learn more about your house and who taught you."

"My house? We were hunters and farmers until the Great War."

"As I said. I would like to hear more about your house." Chazon turned to Abigail. "I must return to the wedding feast. Shammah will wonder where I have gone."

Chazon rubbed his hands on his soiled robe, streaking it further. He shook his head with a rueful expression. "Queen Tamiym gave this to me."

"Our labors with Aleph show upon us." Abigail brushed the dust clinging to her garments.

Chazon chuckled. "They do."

As they made their way toward the palace, Naphtali saw the shopkeeper who saved him and his sister before selling them both. The boy raced ahead. The man looked the same, not any older, but just as aged.

For reasons Naphtali couldn't explain, the man kept them fed and clothed after he found them wandering in the City of Kings. They studied under him, called him uncle, and when Iyar purchased him, Naphtali didn't want to go.

"Uncle, you're still here? I never see you. But you wanted it that way. You sold us. My longing for you eluded your notice."

The man grinned and bowed, his knees creaking as he bent. "Never presume where you lack knowledge, Naphtali. The foolish fall into that pit of trouble every time. Go. Get fresh tunics. You know where to look. Chazon and Lady Abigail will need them so they can return to the wedding feast. You will too."

"You know them?" Naphtali spun toward Chazon and Abigail, then faced the man again. "Who don't you know, Uncle?"

The man's face twinkled. "Ah. What an honor to serve the people while confronting the enemies of Aleph. Are we not called to slay the dragons of the sea and sky, the offspring of the star-born?"

Naphtali's chin drooped. "Uncle, then why not let us stay and learn at your knee? Hulda and I yet weep because of your absence."

The shopkeeper placed a hand on Naphtali's shoulder. Naphtali stiffened as the man held him. "Bend to the strength that flows through you."

CHAPTER SEVEN

TIGERS IN THE GRASSES

Naphtali didn't know what to say to Queen Tamiym, who waited for him to reply to Shammah's question. Now that Abigail had conscripted him to be an apprentice only hours ago, Naphtali didn't know where he belonged.

With Iyar as his master, the boundaries of life revolved around serving the merchant. Naphtali learned Iyar's preferences: how he sucked lamb bones after eating the meat, rose early to review financial tablets, and cooed when he discovered a delicate textile. He had felt the back of Iyar's hand when he failed a task and caught him hiding a smile when Naphtali made him proud.

But Abigail said Naphtali was no longer a slave, a shadow living to the beats of Iyar's whims.

"Young Naphtali, will you not answer?" asked King Shammah. Merriment sprung from him like water from a freshly dug well. "Perhaps the beauty of the queen's presence captivates you. It imprisons me."

The king caught the queen's hand and kissed it. "Distance and longing no longer lie between us, Tamiym. Only love."

Tamiym shouldered closer to Shammah and brushed her lips on his cheek. "May there be grace upon our affection."

Shammah, suddenly sober, kissed Tamiym with the solemnity of a plea. "As it is for our covenant, may it be for the kingdom. How I yearn for overflowing love and peace."

Warmth filled Naphtali's cheeks as he observed the gentleness between the king and queen, while sadness flooded him from heart to bone. Memories of his parents in the Cove of Everlasting, standing at the seashore, clasping hands, nearly triggered tears.

Naphtali felt younger than his ten years, as if he heard the voice of his mother again urging him to protect his sister and to remember how she taught him to be kind and generous. Naphtali cleared his throat and felt his wits return.

He bowed expertly, as Iyar had taught him. "My queen, I entreat your forgiveness. I'm the son of parents slain in the Great War with the Mikana, which you fought valiantly, King Shammah.

"I'm also a former slave to Lord Iyar, where I traveled the deserts and cities here and beyond the kingdom of Seth. Only a short while ago, I became an apprentice for Lady Abigail. Sister of my former master."

"Indeed, you have found prosperity in Lady Abigail's care," Shammah said. "Because it is my wedding day, I will not cite Lord Iyar's difficulties."

Abigail bowed her head at the king's words, while Naphtali inhaled, hoping to quash his stuttering. "My queen, my words are slow in coming because I am struck by this occasion, as the king suggests," he said. "You've brought not only beauty but kindness. I believe, though I am young and unmarried, that when I marry and have sons and daughters, you and the king will not deal falsely with my children or my descendants. For that future, I am grateful."

Tamiym smiled. "And now you have brought kindness to us. Thank you. You also quote a scholar of old when you say we will not deal falsely with your descendants. Young Naphtali, hold us to those words."

Naphtali almost swooned. When the queen spoke directly to him, he remembered the woman petitioning Aleph in the desert outside of Chaniya.

"Lady Abigail, you have a special friend in Naphtali." The king chuckled. "Has the boy ever left Iyar's house? A chick attempting his first steps moves faster than he does."

"Naphtali, do you have more you want to present to us? You are free to speak before the throne," Tamiym said. "No gates restrict you. No one sits in judgment."

Queen Tamiym's lyrical voice rushed through him, and words sprang from him like an arrow. "My lady, were you near the Desert of Akron? Only a few days ago? In the evening?"

"Boy, what do you imply?" Shammah exchanged playfulness for a simmering thunder.

Tamiym leaned forward. "Were you there?"

"My master's caravan stopped in Chaniya. After our evening meal, I walked through the grasses. I heard you praying to Aleph. I didn't know that it was you I overheard."

Tamiym beamed. "What a night beneath Aleph's stars. And we shared it together."

"You stalked my wife like a thief searching for prey during her private petitions," Shammah said. "Perhaps I will send you to a workhouse."

"My lord, let us hear him. Naphtali, did you see two boys that night? They are my brothers. They encountered someone in the desert. A boy their age."

Naphtali gulped. A place of affection with the queen would vanish because of two insolent boys. "It wasn't a happy meeting, my lady. I also saw them here."

Feeling foolish, Naphtali stood closer to Abigail. She wrapped a soothing arm around him. "Naphtali is my friend and apprentice. I am sure the incident was a boyish skirmish."

"Let me ensure this: you will share sweeter greetings," Tamiym said. "None more loyal will you find. Once you get to know them, Naphtali. May I be your friend? Along with my brothers?"

Naphtali couldn't stop the tears that flowed with every memory of the hardships he and his sister faced after their parents died and after the war. How proud his mother would be.

He wiped his face with the back of his hand. "I will serve you for always, my queen. May my sister, Hulda, be your friend? If you don't mind the smell of onions."

Naphtali fell back into his chair with a thud. He rubbed his knees, then his hot, hot cheeks.

"She's wonderful." Naphtali gulped.

Abigail smiled as Naphtali's cheeks slowly cooled. "Queen Tamiym fancies you, Naphtali."

"I hope to meet her again."

"Why my aunt introduced you at all mystifies me." Barak sauntered to their table with that flat voice Naphtali always suspected hid a plot to aggravate someone, usually anyone not born to Barak's aristocratic status.

"No mystery, Nephew," Abigail said. "I'll forgive your rudeness toward Naphtali if you address us properly."

Barak bent and kissed her cheek. He nodded to Naphtali before turning his back toward the boy and settling into a chair.

"Greetings, Aunt Abigail," Barak said.

"Greetings. Where are your siblings?"

"Performing their social duties and representing our father, Iyar, during his illness. Jabin's persuading someone to sell her property. I fear it is not working, though. She clutches her money as her garments show. Could she not spend two extra shekels for more handsome textiles?"

"A swift tongue is a deadly vice." Abigail folded her arms. "What about Keziah?"

"Being escorted through the gardens by three sons of nobles, with their mothers trotting behind them, jerky as hens. None of the three is a candidate. Their wealth will evaporate if one family vessel fails to return. So, as far as I can tell, Jabin and Keziah are both occupied. I doubt they saw you introduce this street vermin to the queen."

Barak stopped his storytelling while raising his hand to Naphtali. "Wine, boy."

The commanding tone was all too familiar. Naphtali jumped up, offered a quick bow, ready to search for the wine jars at the wedding feast.

Abigail stopped Naphtali by gripping the boy's shoulder. "Barak, no more. Naphtali is my apprentice. He is no longer your father's slave. Not another word of insult."

"Apprentice? What can you possibly teach him?"

"Now you insult me."

To Naphtali's surprise, Barak lowered his eyes. No one, not even Iyar, reined in Barak, who slung derogatory phrases like cuts of meat to dogs. Naphtali gazed upward at Abigail, astounded.

Barak bowed before Abigail. "Please forgive me, Aunt Abigail. I did not mean what I said."

"You did mean it. Tigers in the grasses may not be hungry, but they always intend to kill. Practice what I taught you when you were a child. Display kindness."

Barak turned to Naphtali without a trace of snobbishness. "Please forgive me, Naphtali. My congratulations. To sit at my aunt's knee will be an unforgettable privilege."

At that, Abigail touched Barak's cheek and gave him a glimmering smile.

Iyar willed the sickness to flee. Hunched over, he struggled to yell. "Someone bring me more water."

He had to shout because he didn't have Naphtali waiting in a corner to serve him while Iyar abused him with word after word. The remaining slaves stayed in the quarters below when they could, unwilling to linger in Iyar's presence.

It was Barak who came to Iyar's aid. He carried a platter with water and some bread.

"Father, I wish the sickness would leave you. Did you finally send for the physician?"

"All he offers are poultices and promises. It soon will fade. I will wait it out."

"You are strong."

"Not strong enough. Did you see Naphtali with Abigail? I sent him on an errand for the wedding, and he does not return. I will beat him."

"Naphtali has new responsibilities, Father. Aunt Abigail consigned him to her household in Nifla. Tonight. At the wedding."

"As what? A soldier? Naphtali hardly knows east from west. She does not have enough property to need many slaves."

"Aunt Abigail called him her apprentice."

"By the mice," Iyar said. "Whom can I find to replace him? Poor boy. Naphtali would have fared better with me. Rather than follow her path into obscurity and poverty, he may as well have drowned in the Time Sea."

Zalmon snatched the slithering creatures that crawled from bowls and hurled them down his open mouth. Dahv gasped and turned from his plate, choosing to focus on the greenish lights that shone above the ornate table, which was more of an oblong altar, upheld by thick, clawed legs.

Naamah observed him in pity. If not born to the Water People, those from above the waters spent many seasons adjusting to the dim light. Eyesight, skin, and food choices changed. Naamah never ventured from the sea, but she could only imagine Dahv's longings.

She watched as he collected himself and ate one of the boiled fish, avoiding the live sea animals that slid on the table.

"My lord, in these caverns beneath the sea, where does the light originate? And what makes it green as the grasses of Earth?" Dahv asked.

Zalmon pushed a tiny purplish creature into his mouth. It screeched when her father bit into its flesh.

"The star-born built this for us shortly after the waters receded," Zalmon said. "After the Deluge. The light emanates from the jewels they gave us, which enabled us to breathe from under the water. The jewels also allow us to see."

"Power in jewels?"

Zalmon finished chewing with a grunt. "Power beyond our sight or belief."

"Do the Zuzim appear often among the Water People?"

"Often. They've appeared while you've been here. You just didn't know it. But they wanted to ensure your safety with us. Have we not treated you well?"

Dahv bent his head in respect. Naamah didn't have to see his expression to know Dahv had questions about the star-born Zuzim.

"You have, my lord," Dahv said.

"Our gratitude is without end." Mahalath, her father's consort, curled up next to Zalmon's damp body, where beads of water hung, her hair stringy and wet, her lips pouty and red.

Naamah despised the sound of Mahalath's voice. Her father tired of the concubines and wanted her as his queen, but Naamah didn't want Mahalath as a mother. She never knew her mother, only her father. She didn't require any maternal benevolence, which Mahalath lacked. The mothers among her people who threw their sons to the sea horses because they appeared too human showed more loyalty and love. Mahalath vacillated from kindness to testiness, a foul wind from above the waters. She kept her son in another cave, and Naamah wondered why a growing boy couldn't be around others. But her father didn't seem to care, so Naamah never asked.

Dahv folded his arms and delivered a straightforward gaze to Mahalath. "Glorious power. Can nothing compete with it?"

"Nothing," Mahalath said.

The king stood up and placed his muscled arms on his hips as he scanned the table.

"I will marry Mahalath. She will be my queen."

Naamah gathered enough self-possession not to gasp and scream.

"Blessings from Livnath," said Qayin. "This union will birth a new prosperity."

"Blessings," Haran muttered as he continued to eat.

Naamah waited for Dahv's response. With arms still folded, face inscrutable, and his voice thick, Dahv said, "Blessings. More power for your throne."

"Livnath approves of the union," said the king. "Do you question it?"

Dahv unlocked his arms and leaned forward. "What plans does this union foreshadow for my people in Seth?"

The king roared with laughter, but not from revelry. An edge of a spear lay within his bellows. Naamah didn't shudder at the sound, but she worried Dahv would forfeit the opportunity to be accepted by her father.

Zalmon stood at his full height, touching nearly the ceiling. His yellow eyes blinked rhythmically, matching the gaze of the spotted yellow fish swimming in nearby feeding waters.

"Here is what I choose to tell you. Not only will I wed, but so will you, Dahv. Your union will inaugurate a new line for the throne of Seth once I and the star-born overtake it. We've already begun the first steps to undermine its strength under Shammah."

"Father, we have not discussed this." Naamah tried to bridle excitement. Musings from her heart had become reality.

Dahv never looked at Naamah but bowed to Zalmon. "Your will."

"Of course, it is," Zalmon said. "The sitting king, the brother you refuse to claim, the man you usurped, the man who defeated you, the man who sits on Seth's throne, killed my son."

Zalmon pulled a dagger from his belt. It glinted in the green light. "With this, Shammah killed my son, and with it, I will throw him as meat to the sea dragon."

Dahv bowed again. "Your will, King Zalmon. Hatred for Shammah propelled me to the throne. Hatred demands I return."

This time, the king's laughter was genuine. "Then, very good. My daughter is your betrothed. Return to your seat. Naamah, sit beside your future husband. I'm eager to watch the sea horses play."

Dahv said nothing as the human-sized sea horses paraded from underneath the pond, first appearing as black, then turning to a slight red as they marched along the shoreline, arranging themselves into companies. They bowed to each other in respect and sparred with swords and sickles.

"Once our enemies, now our sport," Naamah whispered to Dahv.

"As any enemy should be." He reached for her hand and kissed it. "My expectations rise, knowing you understand this."

Naamah resisted throwing herself into his arms.

Green mist clouded Dahv's sight, but when the slaves arrived, he wished he couldn't see at all. An enormous fish bounced on a platter the slaves hoisted on their shoulders. The hooded pupils of the fish blinked alive, and the red scales seemed fresh as blood. Bitterness rose in Dahv's mouth.

Two slaves cut the fish in half and thrust it into a hot grate on the table. The fish head, looking far from dead, they left on the platter facing Dahv.

After a few minutes, the slaves placed the fish halves on the table, revealing thick pink-and-white chunks of flesh.

Naamah cooed, grabbed a chunk of fish, and stuffed it into her mouth. She licked her fingers.

"Sweet."

"I am accustomed to smaller carp. What fish is this?"

A blush coated Naamah's cheeks as she stroked the fishtail. "It's a rare beast that originates from the deep. It doesn't swim in the higher waters. We search for it only at marriage ceremonies."

Slaves added seaweed, cabbage, and turnips to the table. With a yelp, Dahv snatched a turnip and a fistful of cabbage. "Where did these come from?"

"I asked the slaves to find food from above ground as a wedding present."

Dahv bit into the turnip, drooling as he crunched. "No greater gift could you have chosen."

He reached for the cabbage to stuff his mouth further but paused when a steel-gray light lit the cave's opening, causing the green mist to lift. The slapping noise of wet skin sliding against rock walls followed the light.

"What is that?" Dahv said.

"The special fish, and this wedding cave, are the gifts of the sea dragon. He doesn't always appear at nuptials. When he does, the visit expresses his pleasure. He favors us. Can you not feel the wonder of it? The star-born has placed his approval on us."

"A sea dragon?" Dahv spit out the turnip and reached for his dagger. But Dahv had lived in caves for years and lost disciplines; he hadn't tied his dagger to his waist.

Dahv backed up from the table, stretching out an arm to protect Naamah. She shook off his arm; her lips parted as the dragon entered, not gushing fire but reeking of water. Gurgled breaths from the beast echoed in the cave.

"Our people first saw the sea dragon after the Great Deluge," Naamah said. "Some believe it lived before the waters flooded. Others say it was born from the floodwaters and never has known Earth."

"I care nothing about the wretched womb that brought it forth. Will it kill us?"

"No, but with his appearance, the dragon intends to bind us to him forever."

"Why would I want that? Why?"

Naamah placed a hand on his thigh. "Quiet."

The dragon widened its mouth and black-and-gray bitumen mixed with foamy water seeped between spiked teeth. The dragon rocked its head and flapped its short wings. Dahv couldn't look away. Then he heard a scream. It was his own.

He twisted his thigh beneath Naamah's grip, unable to break free.

"Wait," she said. Naamah's soothing voice deepened into a growl, and he turned to her in surprise. She sat rigid as a watcher in a tree.

The dragon continued the rocking motion, swallowed, and opened its jaws within a hand's span of Dahv and Naamah. Odors of decay spilled into Dahv's nostrils.

Dahv shrank back. Naamah's nails dug into his thigh until blood seeped from his leg beneath his tunic. With her free hand, Naamah placed a chunk of fish from their table into the dragon's mouth. The dragon's coiling tongue lapped up the fish with a swish of dirty water.

The dragon tilted his head toward Dahv, blood-shot eyes examining him. With a shallow heave, Dahv tossed fish chunks inside the dragon's mouth then tore Naamah's hand from his thigh while shoving his body from the table and flattening himself against the cave wall.

"I am the *tannin* that defied the waters, and the waters to come." The dragon gurgled the words in a muffled roar.

Fiery red scales glowed on the dragon's body until they melted away, revealing a thin, grayish man with a sunken face. With a trembling arm, beneath heavily embroidered robes of gold and blue mildewed by sea foam, the dragon-man pointed toward Dahv.

"Aleph snatched my glory from the stars, hurled me into the Time Sea, and bound me in this body, but I possess power and will."

Lullabies never sounded softer. Because of the diminutive volume of the dragon's voice, he sounded like a mother murmuring to a babe. Dahv relaxed.

The man threw a blood-red gaze at Dahv before dropping his arm. "The cities my companions built on the shores of the Time Sea lie buried beneath the waters. My offspring once lived in palaces, long before Zalmon, my son. Aleph herded us into underwater caves, locked away from our homes and wealth. Through you, we will open the gates of the sea and return to our cities."

"Through me?"

"Hatred unlocks the gates. Because of you, Dahv of Seth, I will be able to say, 'His heel crushes me, but I will ascend.'"

Each word, like poisoned arrows, pierced Dahv's soul. Dahv peeled himself from the cavern wall.

He raised his right hand and green fire surged from shoulder to fingertips. Eagerness soared through him, along with the thirst for war. After years of cold and dankness, the dragon-man revived Dahv's flaccid body and dead hopes and set them ablaze.

"His heel crushes me," Dahv repeated with the eagerness of a newly recruited defender. "But I will ascend."

"Your first task. Replace the tablets into the wall behind you."

Dahv swung around. Behind him were two empty niches.

"Then capture a third tablet and carve a niche for it in that wall. When the time comes to fulfill your tasks, I will call you," the dragon-man said.

The fiery scales fanned around the man and enclosed him once more. The dragon returned. It cawed in bursts that jerked his body until rocks fell from the walls of the cave.

"We leave now." Naamah grabbed Dahv's hand, and they raced from the cave.

When they finally stopped at one of the more familiar tunnels, she let him go. Dahv struggled to inhale air while rubbing his right wrist and fingers. "My sword hand. What did that green fire do to my sword hand?"

Naamah, flushing and twirling her arms, appeared rejuvenated. "He affirmed your covenant with him. Our covenant."

"We are the last couple," Dahv said. "The beast destroyed the cave."

Naamah's face became more fish-like. Her appearance nearly sickened him. "The destruction represents an agreement.

He'll restore the cave for a future nuptial. Each time he meets with our people, he destroys the cave. The destruction appears worse than ever because we lost the tablets, and he seethes over it. We bound ourselves to him, my husband. We must obey all he asks."

"What tablets must we return to the Water People? Why do they matter to that creature?"

"We won't speak of them now. But in time. My father assigned this task to the high priest, Ezer, along with a few minions. But if the high priest fails, we cannot."

"Of course," Dahv said. "I am also curious about this. How did Mahalath respond when she married your father? What did she think of the dragon-man? Did he approve of their union?"

Dahv didn't wait for an answer but pinched his nose in distaste. "Sewage. Where did that odor come from? We left that foul cave."

Nausea filled his nostrils, and he bent over as if absorbing blows from an unseen assailant.

Naamah smiled, shiny and hard. "Mahalath never saw what we witnessed. I urge you to lose every grain of affection for her."

Dahv reached for Naamah with a groan. "Help me. What is this sickness, wife?"

She sidestepped him and spoke over her shoulder. "The sickness will pass in a few moments," she said. "I'll command the slaves to fetch you fresh water."

Dahv gaped at her, gagging for pure air and Earth.

Ezer slouched in his chair, slightly hidden by the growing night darkness. He didn't light the oil lamps because he refused to observe Qatsar binding his wounds because they shouted his humiliation.

Several days ago, Ezer had crouched before King Zalmon, explaining why the sacrifice of oxen at Livnath's temple ruins hadn't upended Shammah's nuptials, why Livnath couldn't manifest into this world as she wished, and why he didn't have the tablets. When Ezer offered answers that didn't satisfy Zalmon, the king summoned a sea horse to snatch two of the high priest's fingers from his right hand.

Ezer's news about what happened at Livnath's temple deepened Zalmon's anger because the king had betrothed his daughter to Dahv. The king of the Water People had anticipated a double victory against the kingdom of Seth, but Ezer had failed him.

"I could have fared worse," Ezer said to Qatsar.

"Yes, my lord," Qatsar said. "If Zalmon hadn't reined in the creature with his whip, the sea horse would have gnawed your arm."

Qatsar's ears suddenly burned red while he wrapped Ezer's hand carefully, added a sour-smelling ointment, then washed his hands in a bowl. "High priest, if you would allow me to speak once more."

"Go on."

"I believe, I suspect—I know who took the tablets from us. It wasn't Iyar himself, however, I've traced the culprit to his house."

"Who is it?"

"A slave who once worked for the man we assigned to remove the tablets from Iyar's home. She can lead us to them. She is called Hulda."

Ezer sighed. "May she be as her name. An insignificant mole or weasel. Stay close to her."

"We need not rush to capture her. She recently arrived at Iyar's house and could open the gates to many possibilities. Allow me to build a friendship with the cook Levi. It will take time, but I expect it to yield fruit."

CHAPTER EIGHT

THE VULTURES

The vultures appeared during Tamiym's ninth month, weeks before the strain of delivery arrived. They boasted wingspans that blotted small clouds. No animal carcasses or refuse could have drawn the vultures. No beleaguered army marched with injured and dying soldiers, and yet the death eaters hung in the air, hungry for flesh and thirsty for blood.

They circled for an hour over the palace, never escaping the chief midwife's sight. Tamiym had hired Shiphrah because she was the mistress of a thousand childbirths. Women throughout the kingdom of Seth whispered in awe when they heard her name. One story boasted how Shiphrah cuddled a babe who had nearly drowned in the womb. Another claimed she mourned with the mother for days when the life cord strangled her little one.

Shiphrah, the eldest daughter of a family near the Cove of Revealing, the seaport city of dolphins and sea monsters, was the last of a midwives' guild from southern Seth. Never did Shiphrah babble about the gods or appear vexed like the younger midwives serving at the palace. Bringing mortals into the world held Shiphrah's attention. But the morning the vultures descended, the famed midwife sought an audience with the queen. The vultures ignited a worry Shiphrah couldn't overlook. The birds of prey were another omen, and she expected Tamiym's delivery to be difficult.

Clutching her walking stick, the midwife held her lips in a thin, worried line. "The vultures promise rebirth only to those who worship her."

"I express no such devotion."

"Because of that, she intends to kill your babes."

Tamiym walked to the balcony overlooking the City of Kings. Smoke rose from fires where families roasted meat and vegetables for evening meals and unfurled sleeping mats on their rooftops. Every decision she made about her delivery, Tamiym knew, would affect them.

"The moon goddess has declared war."

Shiphrah shifted her weight on her stick. While the stick's battered wood showed its age, the midwife's face bore no wrinkles. Only strands of gray streamed her wavy hair.

"Once I delivered a son who died as he slipped from his mother's womb into my hands. I hadn't wiped the blood from his face before he perished. I learned later that the babe's mother had cursed Livnath during her sixth month.

"The mother's marriage was souring. She blamed Livnath for the collapsing union, reviling the name and power of the goddess. I never saw Livnath at the birth bricks, but I felt her presence. Coldness and hate wrapped around the babe. Even the mother's birthing sweat turned to shivers. Livnath killed the babe with the slap of her open hand. That mother was young, ungrateful, and foolish. When I saw the vultures, my fears took root. I beg you, Queen Tamiym. What is your answer?"

"Aleph."

The chief midwife pushed a sigh from her lips. "As you say."

Her walking stick thudded on the stone floor as Shiphrah, shoulders slumped, turned to leave.

On her left side, Tamiym felt kicking. The queen massaged where she felt the movement. "Peace, little warrior. Aleph will fight for us."

When Tamiym awakened the next morning, the younger midwives sat outside her chambers. Tamiym folded her hands across her belly and studied the four women. One was born in the City of Kings, another from Arba. Two hailed from Nifla. Each was unmarried. So far, they had served Shiphrah at only a hundred births between them, but the chief midwife chose them because of their potential to attend to many mothers to come.

"Shiphrah sent you?"

The tallest, Puah, a woman from Nifla, nodded. "She is journeying to the north to attend another birth. She returns tomorrow. She wants us to serve you closely, my lady. Please ask us for anything. Please."

Throughout the day, the midwives shadowed Tamiym's steps. They trailed when she waddled to a chamber table or stumbled to a bench. Although they knew she would refuse them, they urged Tamiym to place fertility amulets beneath her pillows, sip potions, and wear images of rival gods who could protect her from Livnath's ire.

They followed behind her, chirping sparrows who didn't know how to stop offering advice. Finally, Tamiym raised her right hand. "No more. All I require is help to prepare my body for birth."

Silenced, Puah blushed as she, and the other midwives, bowed before the queen.

The next day, the women hovered in palace corners and at the edge of the Gardens of Destiny as Tamiym read tablets among patches of flowers. As much as they could, they gave her a narrow space of solitude.

Everything in Tamiym longed to journey to Aleph and wait for more revelation from the Existing One. But it wasn't time. Traveling was unsafe. Already, fatigue came quickly. And as she strolled from the gardens, she smiled. She longed for a nap.

When she reached her chamber, Shammah entered as she sat on the bed. The warmth in his eyes stretched toward her, carving a warm path like sunlight. Tamiym's thoughts about napping fled.

When he kneeled to kiss her belly, she curled her right fingers through his thick braids of hair.

"Your afternoon visits are to check on your heir, not me."

He kissed her belly again before looking up at Tamiym's face. "The midwives say 'heirs,' and I believe them. And, of course, I must watch over them as they prepare for this world while making sure my queen prepares for them. I expect them to be rambunctious, full of dreams and ambitions, lovers of learning, and children who serve the Existing One and his people."

Tamiym gave him a lopsided smile. "You sing songs to us all, and we listen."

"As long as you heed my voice."

She wondered if he would heed hers. She never openly agreed with the midwives that she probably carried twins. The possibility of two babes after praying for one child filled her heart with delight, but she feared what she desired.

Tamiym also restrained herself from telling Shammah about her night visions. She couldn't identify their gender, but she saw two babes lying close to her. The visions rambled through her mind, but she couldn't tell Shammah yet. She wanted to see them alive and present them to him as her gift before releasing the joy blossoming within her.

Tamiym bent to kiss his hair. "I listen to you, my love."

"Speak that again. The Queen of Seth listens to the king. Does she listen because my lips touch her hair or because my lips touch her cheek?"

Shammah's protective love washed over her. He stood. "Since the queen pledges to listen, then you will not mind meeting with the noble families tomorrow, if you are not too weary. I understand the time comes soon."

"The babes are heavy to carry, but I know these gatherings are important."

"But not to you, Tamiym."

"Pretensions bore me. Spending time with the scribes, the children, and the farmers, even Peleg and his oily merchants, seems more worthwhile to entertain."

"Which is why I want you by my side. The noble families need to draw from your wisdom. Only new learning will guide them from closed, backward ways. The Great War altered their perspectives, at least for a moment.

"But these few years of peace led some back to old, selfish, and corrupted things. The lack of insight and purpose among the aristocratic women pains you the most, I think."

"Perhaps. But your conversation always refreshes me," Tamiym said.

She didn't want to admit feeling less of a queen and more like the artisan farmer's daughter and Chaniyan scholar. Life in her home city involved befriending toddlers and those restless for learning.

In the City of Kings, she politely sparred with the self-absorbed rich who inherited the rare chance to be literate and withheld it from the poor while ignoring the slights of noblewomen who feigned sickness or deafness in her presence to show their distaste about her humble origins.

To needle Tamiym, the women complimented each other about their hair jewels, robes, and perfumes, but never glanced at the queen. She was a warrior-woman with firm hands and height, glowing eyes the color of bear fur, crinkly, braided hair she forced into place, and she declined their invitations to rooftop gatherings or purification rituals for Livnath.

With a hand to her back, Tamiym rose from the bed to place her head on Shammah's chest. "My love, where you go, I go."

While Tamiym no longer wore the rough robes of her station in Chaniya and donned the well-cut garments of Shammah's queen, she refused to boast about textiles and lapis lazuli, as many of the noblewomen did. One of them, a petite woman wearing an intricate headdress, parted from her husband and approached Tamiym.

"The embroidery on your gown is the envy of the room," the woman said. She reached out to touch a hem until she remembered Tamiym was the queen, not a neighbor.

"Thank you," Tamiym said. "The artisan has a booth in the southern sector. Perhaps you have noticed her? A humble booth is all she has, but her skills rival all."

The woman dug her hands beneath her tunic and tossed her head, causing the headdress to bob.

"The bazaar? I thought the queen imported garments from Edrei or perhaps Midvar. Why wear what everyone else has? I bought this headdress from a craftswoman in Edrei."

"And your headdress is a rarity in any gathering," Tamiym said.

The woman crinkled her lips and nose in a smug expression before drifting to a stylish woman like herself, who draped her curves with a sesame-colored sash and long fringe.

Tamiym sighed. She could read three languages, do calculations without tablets, decipher complicated business transactions, and recite kings' lists, and that knowledge felt like weights when she mingled with the noblewomen who frequented the palace.

Every word revealed the indolence of their lifestyles. Never guided as women to learn a trade, survive a drought, or to find shelter, they relaxed with gossip, created rivalries between their houses, and shared rare wines in the afternoon to pass the time. They suffocated Tamiym with their idleness.

Before she could escape to the balcony, Shammah touched her shoulder.

"My love. Do not bear the burden of peacocks."

Tamiym smiled. "Was my frustration apparent?"

"Only Aleph sees everything. But as your humble husband, Aleph has given me some sight."

Shammah kissed her cheek as another noblewoman, Liraz, bowed before them. "My king and queen, I wanted to introduce you to Lady Kerem. She arrived recently from Yaphah. King Aikah's home city."

Kerem bowed. "King Shammah, Queen Tamiym, it is an honor."

"Welcome, Lady Kerem," Shammah said. "I hope you have settled into your new home?"

"Just barely, my lord."

"What is your family's trade?"

"Vineyards. Our ancestral houses were two of the first to cultivate vines. If you allow us, I would like to send our best wines."

Tamiym noticed the slight scars on the woman's hands. "Do you work as a vinedresser along with your husband?"

Kerem nodded. "Once. No more. As we prospered, my husband wanted me to work less and to have children. We moved to the City of Kings to rear them in the best scribal schools."

"How children many do you have?" Shammah smiled.

"None as yet."

"By the grace of Aleph, may it be soon," Shammah said.

"I waited for a year," Tamiym said. "May you know my gratefulness."

Kerem blushed. "Waiting wearies me. I cannot toil among the vines, and the days in the house have left me wanting."

The exchange bored Liraz, who Tamiym knew never labored a moment because both her father and husband's houses were part of the nobility. All the children Liraz had borne were adults, and childbearing lay far behind her.

"My lord is from Nifla," Liraz said to Kerem. "So is my house."

"I was young there. I do not fully know or remember it." Shammah shifted his attention to Kerem. "Is your husband with you?"

"Not tonight, my lord. He sends regrets he could not attend. Business called him to Chaniya."

"The queen is from Chaniya," Liraz lowered her voice so that only Tamiym could hear.

Tamiym stood stiffly as Liraz fawned before the king.

"My lord, I will make sure you meet Lady Kerem's husband," Liraz said.

Shammah nodded at Liraz but directed his words to Kerem. "My lady, Yaphah is the home of King Aikah and the new home of Gila, the queen mother. It would be an honor for my queen to host you and your husband. Send a messenger to the palace when your husband returns."

Kerem bowed. "An honor, my lord. An honor."

As the two women drifted away, Tamiym tucked her arm into Shammah's. "You saw that."

"If we can encourage a couple who longs for children," Shammah said, "we will do it even in the face of snobbishness from Liraz. She's a noblewoman who has forgotten when she longed for babes to hold and the days before she could enter the palace doors."

Peleg sauntered toward them before bowing with a flourish. "You inspired Lady Kerem. Well, so am I, as always."

"Peleg, you place a thin veil over your sarcasm," Tamiym said.

"My apologies. I wanted my lady to know that they are not all like Lady Liraz."

"Indeed," Shammah said. "Peleg, please stay with the queen for a few moments before we start the feast."

Peleg shouldered a spot beside Tamiym, appearing as formidable as one of the palace guards.

"The noblewoman who condescends to the queen and misleads the newcomer has created a widespread reputation by demeaning others," Peleg said. "People behave uprightly but distant from her because they fear being clawed by her hateful snippets. Many circles have abandoned nobles who've reached this woman's libelous shores. Breathe a wrong word, and she hears and condemns. Anytime I hear her ill-meaning observations, my wager is always on the person she disparages. My lady, I have more trust in the faithful invasion of grain mites every harvest than I do the faithless words of this woman."

Peleg's voice dropped to a whisper. "Shammah needed to marry you. No one else. Like you, Mahalath was beautiful. She was also well-studied, the offspring of a very-connected house that descends from the sacred founding, but useless. When it was time to emerge from the Great War as the valiant betrothed of King Shammah, she emerged as a conspirator of the star-born. As we all have speculated, she languishes like a worm beneath the Time Sea. Yes, I am a devotee of Livnath, and I've never hid that, but Mahalath fought for the wrong side in the war. If circumstances had turned out differently, more than likely, Mahalath would rule Seth alongside Dahv, another rebel. My imagination drags me to dreadful places when I consider them as king and queen. Again, Shammah needed to marry you."

"Thank you, Peleg, but I shouldn't be grateful. I should reprove you. Seth's queen must be a neutral voice for every citizen. A protector for the kingdom."

"We'll revisit that at my next lesson, my lady. You can't be neutral in the face of excesses that burden the poor incessantly and without cause. You must make allegiances."

She nodded. Peleg's intervention boosted her spirits and enabled her to shelve misgivings about being queen for another day.

Three evenings later, Iyar hosted a gathering of customers, nobles who sought the jewels, textiles, or spices he brought in by caravan from Edrei or Midvar. If they weren't customers, they were longtime friends from noble families who relished his gatherings because he offered the best dishes in the City of Kings in the finest house. Many of them also owed him money or had borrowed so often they hung their heads when they entered his courtyard.

Iyar knew everyone was still talking about the palace gathering, which he had decided not to attend. He wanted to test where loyalties stood for the king by getting his influential friends to share openly. Getting their fill of wine and food would open their minds and hearts.

Usually, he tormented them, delighting in flaunting his wealth and making them suffer. But now he had amassed enough of their money and his cruelties wearied him. As he greeted friends in the well-dressed crowd, he couldn't help but remember how the visit from the four desert horsemen had changed everything.

Chaggay came up to him, his breath heavy with one of Iyar's Yaphah wines. He tapped Iyar on his chest, flushed with merriment. "Another satisfying feast, Iyar."

Iyar stepped back from him, annoyed, though his face didn't reveal it. "My pleasure, Chaggay. Have you sampled all from my table? There is a special dish of dates you may like."

Chaggay tapped him on the chest again. "No. No. More. Food. Can you see I have had enough?"

The noble hiccupped and kept talking. "I am angry with you. Gossips have told me you seek to buy the land of Livnath's ruined temple. I want to do that. It's precious land, and the priests have done little to it despite their architects and markings."

"Maybe they choose altars in caves and grasses throughout Seth because not enough of Livnath's followers want to spend their lives hewing pitch and tone for her," Iyar said.

"I want to build there. For the goddess. For the priests. What do you want with it?" When Chaggay placed his finger on Iyar's chest again, this time, Iyar was less restrained. He gripped Chaggay's hand and lowered it to the man's side.

"I never share my business intentions. You have known me too long to forget that."

"That's what bothers me. Why would a wealthy merchant long for Livnath's ruined temple?" Chaggay waved his arm toward the courtyard. "Feasts and goods from faraway kingdoms no one else will visit or even desire to see. You are not so homebound to claim an interest in a temple and far from humble to bow to the skies."

Iyar kept his face immobile. He must keep his self-indulgent reputation intact.

He offered a mock bow. "Can we all not change and mature?"

"We can, but you will not," interrupted E-ven, another noble.

"Place reins on his neck, E-ven. He is an ox who has broken away from his cart." Chaggay sauntered away, hailing a slave for more wine.

Unlike Chaggay, E-ven wasn't drunk in the slightest, though Iyar wished he were. With E-ven was his wife, Mara. Only in recent years had they reappeared in social circles. After their daughter Mahalath disgraced herself at her wedding feast with King Shammah with her tawdry bride clothes and her admission that she carried a babe fathered by a Zuzim, Mahalath's parents secluded themselves from their friends.

The scandal marred the respect their house once commanded as descendants of one of the first families of the City of Kings, but E-ven desperately wanted to rebuild it.

"E-ven," Iyar said, lightly holding the man's arm before bowing before Mara. "Thank you for visiting my home."

The dullness from that outlandish wedding day draped Mara's face, but she attempted a smile. "Iyar, your home is lovely. And your children? How are they?"

"We didn't come to the feast to discuss offspring, Wife," Ev-en said.

Mara's tentative smile dissolved into a grim line. "I can speak as I please."

"Perhaps. But not now."

Iyar, put off by the coldness emanating from E-ven, lavished a smile on Mara. "They are well, Lady Mara."

"Why are you interested in the ruined temple?" E-ven pressed. "It should not be purchased or sold."

"Should it remain in ruins, my lord? Why tolerate an eyesore," Iyar said. "Should not a business owner like you not invest?"

E-ven grimaced and Iyar knew what that meant. E-ven's wealth had diminished since the Mahalath's departure. "I do not share your blatant greed for more land, Iyar, and I oppose your efforts. Let the gods care for their sacred lands. It's theirs, not ours. The only opportunist I fear more would be the king if the king desired the temple site for one of his massive projects."

Once the guests left, Iyar settled his bulk into a chair. He longed for his father. He never could hear Yissak's stories enough because they caused him to dream and hope. As he was growing into puberty, thieves robbed and killed Yissack on one of those evenings when the day gave way to night.

The tragedy plunged Iyar's family into despair and unwound the closeness they enjoyed. His mother remarried a foul-mouthed scribe who whittled joy from the household. He beat Iyar and his brother when he got drunk and berated their mother and sister with words about their cooking and their lack of learning.

Nothing about his new family pleased the scribe, except the money he collected from the properties Iyar's father owned. The law wouldn't allow Iyar's mother to assume ownership of her husband's property, so she married the brutish scribe to keep their family home. Her sufferings left her sickly and bound to her bed and unable to protect her children from the scribe's vices.

The scribe fell ill suddenly when Iyar was old enough to take up his father's trade and keep his family financially secure without the scribe's help. Iyar remembered how his emergence as a man seemed to weaken the scribe, perhaps because the man feared the young men he bullied as boys, and his worries caused him to loiter in the taverns with other scribes.

One of the scribe's friends accused him of stealing money and poisoned him. After several painful days, the scribe died, and Iyar's family rejoiced. Their happiness was short-lived. Their ancestral home burned down during a drought. A few months later, saddened by the loss of her husband Yissack's home, Mother died from an illness.

The years with the scribe hardened Iyar. In ways he hated to admit, he had assumed the man's selfish arrogance. The property was Iyar's as the elder son, and he squandered it and left little for his siblings. Iyar yearned for acclaim, as did the scribe his mother married, and he received it.

Hulda entered the room with a platter of bread and wine. Iyar gave her a slight smile. Abigail's suggestion that he bring her to his house was a splendid one. Hulda was a fabulous cook, and her wit and plainspoken observations protected him as Naphtali's earnestness and loyalty had.

"We will have to refresh the pantries," Hulda said. "Your friends devoured the food like birds fighting for seeds. I longed to dash through the courtyard and shoo each one away."

He sipped on the wine Hulda poured for him. "If you came to pluck a compliment from me, you will not get it. I do not praise my daughter. Why would I commend a slave?"

"But I am not a slave, my lord. Shall I fetch my contract tablet? You pay me good wages for running your kitchen under Cook Levi's guidance. Lady Abigail made sure of that."

Mara unwound the sleeping wrap on her head, revealing the sparse hairs that sprung from her scalp, a remnant of former glory. She combed a few hairs with her fingers, careful not to lose those that were left. When she was a young woman, unmarried and full of hopes, Mara's hair waved around her throat and curled along her spine. Black tendrils framed her soft jaw and cheeks with a tint of rose.

Hope evaporated when Mara married, a woman barely out of her teens who bore two daughters and endured the constant weight of being a part of a noble house. E-ven boasted at every chance about his inheritance and his family's descending from the founding of the kingdom and that one of his female ancestors was a queen. Her parents cherished the arranged union and felt themselves kissed by the goddess Livnath that E-ven had chosen her. What they didn't know was that E-ven struggled to be kind. When someone crossed him or fell from his expectations, he responded with a whip of words and social insults.

With every year, Mara's hair lost more strands. Her soft jaw dropped to a wrinkled curve. Yellowish skin shades replaced the tint of rose.

She could blame her lost beauty on E-ven and his insistence that they attend every royal feast or how he forced her to pummel their eldest daughter Mahalath with preparations to be queen because he knew King Aikah would choose her to be Shammah's wife. Circumstances proved E-ven right, but his ambition cost them deeply. Neither of them recognized Mahalath's vulnerability, her fragility, and her longing for acceptance.

A strand of gray hair slid to Mara's lap, joining in memory the clumps of hair that had fallen from her since Mahalath left. Instead of weeping, Mara became despondent. She struggled beneath weights of humiliation because of Mahalath's departure and E-ven's fury over it. Rina, her youngest, visited rarely, choosing to build a life away from them.

By an unspoken pact, Mara and E-ven waded through life in pain, shorn of their daughters. They would have remained in that place until recently, when E-ven learned that Iyar was considering purchasing the ruined temple of Livnath. Something inside of E-ven shattered like a trampled twig. He insisted on attending Iyar's feast several nights ago. Throughout the evening, he huddled near the high priest. The friendship didn't surprise Mara; it annoyed her. Ezer walked in arrogance but cloyed when needed. Whenever he visited, Mara complained of headaches and stayed in her bed and greeted him briefly whenever they met.

The sparse hairs were in place. Mara chose another head wrap, bright yellow with a few precious stones threaded into the fabric. E-ven entered the chamber with a grunt. "Wife."

"Yes, Husband?"

"Our plans are taking shape. I believe Iyar's eldest son will ally with us."

"Is he a worshipper of Livnath? I don't remember him at the temple rituals or visiting the neighborhood altars."

"Does it matter? If he supports us, this increases our chances of defeating Iyar. When we meet with the priests, they will tell us how to outwit Iyar in the council-court. Wealth doesn't always conquer."

"But he has so much of it."

E-ven scowled at her. "But we have the family line. We descend from Tapel, remember? The esteemed elder during the sacred founding, remember? What does Iyar have? His line is a wretched disappointment. The house of Iyar birthed rich rebels who defied the gods. Iyar's house will wander even in the grave. It is a privilege to battle for Livnath."

"What about our daughters? Livnath destroyed our family with a swing of her robe. I could send searches for Rina. The high priest could let us know about Mahalath, could he not? Why do you slow your steps when I mention the bone of our bones? Does not your heart break like mine?"

E-ven tightened his jaw. "The first fault lies with you. Did you not fail to bear a son to perpetuate my famous house? I shoulder that shame every day. As far as Mahalath, the goddess carried her on a path that did not take her to the palace as we planned. I bow to Livnath's decision. And Rina? She abandoned us. You will not pursue a child who fled her parents. But you and me? We are loyal to the goddess. Loyal. I command you to remember it."

Iyar didn't know whether to scream her name or whisper it. He missed her. He hated her. But here she was, his beloved Abigail, strolling in his courtyard, her head upraised, unimpressed by his expensive textiles, the silver, gold, and copper in his furniture and utensils. Where his guests fawned only days ago, she ignored. She found a simple bench near his grove of olive trees.

"Hulda's presence has made a difference, even in the courtyard. She sees where you cannot."

He wiped an invisible crumb from his table in the courtyard. "You stole Naphtali, you kept the tablets, you did not deliver them to the king, you put my slave's sister on my payroll, and now you come to me."

Abigail joined him at the table. "No crumbs are there. You always fight when there is no battle, and pursue combat when there is no war. How I loved you, as did our parents and brother."

"You owe me a gesture of repentance."

"I have wronged you, Brother. Please forgive me. I took Naphtali away to protect him and to guide him into his destiny. I presented Hulda to you for her protection and Naphtali's peace. The shopkeeper kept the tablets until we prepared a place for them in Nifla. I also have not told you how much I love you and how my heart aches for you."

"Why? That confounded sickness fled a few months after the king married the queen two years ago. I have never discovered its source, however."

"Yet sickness remains. Do the torments still afflict you?"

"Sister. There is a wall even you cannot cross."

"As you remind me. I pray for them to fade as you walk in Aleph's intentions. You have your instructions from the Gabar and the *malakim*. But I have no sense of the time. Do you? Have you arranged to purchase the ruins now that we know the truth?"

"I have. I cannot prove it, and he refuses to come see me, but the rumors say my son opposes me."

"Jabin's soul has been twisted since—"

"Do not say it."

"When is the date of the sale?"

"Any day now, unless the king opposes it."

"Have you prepared for the resistance?"

"Do you mean have I readied myself for star-born enemies to destroy my possessions and then take my life? Maybe not. Maybe I like my life. Maybe I even love it. The rats that crawl on foul meat left in the streets love their lives. Why cannot I love mine?"

"Because you are Iyar, the son of generations of Iyars, and you must ensure that the City of Kings remains in the possession of Aleph and that Shammah remains its king."

Jabin, incensed, paced in his father's courtyard. He felt stifled within his father's home and even more in his father's presence, a gathering cloud that had suffocated him as long as he could remember. Iyar wielded a scepter of demands while he lived the life of a lout who cared little for anyone else.

While pacing the courtyard, Jabin avoided gazing directly at Iyar. He sought to shield himself from the usual barbs and cursing Father tossed at him like a boy at play. Even with his father's claim of repenting from his old ways, Jabin doubted he ever would, and he longed to throttle his father's desire for righteousness. Men didn't change. They worsened in character, employing new guises, and clothing themselves in fresh forms of unholiness.

Iyar hadn't changed either. His father had discovered another weapon to trigger resentment.

"Buying the temple ruins is ludicrous, Father. Chaggay sings about the foolishness of your pursuit to his friends," Jabin said. "You will enrage the priests and perhaps Livnath herself. Do you want the goddess trampling your goods and property?"

Iyar squatted his bulk on a stool and bit into a date. "Concerns for my safety? Unexpected indeed."

"Father, do not traipse around the issue. Your bid is repulsive and foolish."

"Your inheritance is intact."

"But my name is there."

"You are not an Iyar."

"Another blow to me, your firstborn son. Why do I not carry the name of our house?"

"Your mother hated the name."

"I have never believed that excuse."

"Your folly."

Jabin snorted and felt uncomely. He plopped on a stool. He looked upward, counted the beams in the well-crafted ceiling, and blinked several times. Self-possession seeped from him like milk from a cracked jar. Every memory he had of his father revolved around catching a thread of his attention.

When he was a boy and needed his father to toss a ball with him in the courtyard, Iyar refused because he busily stacked coins. When Jabin wanted to travel with his father on a caravan, Iyar denied him, saying he didn't have the stomach to negotiate with merchants and lacked the strength to face a desert pirate along the way. Whenever Jabin sought Iyar, his father fled, a waft of smoke that refused to remain.

Years with Iyar had taught Jabin how to grow without him and maneuver among the noble classes and build his own alliances. Jabin owned an ornate home and slaves like his father. At this moment, when the calluses from his boyhood threatened to rupture, Jabin remembered what he had achieved without his father. The nobles held him in high regard for his financial decisions. Several families longed for him to choose a bride from their houses. Jabin gained that reputation on his own.

"The priests will sabotage you when you present your bid to the nobles and elders," Jabin said. "They may force the king to step in."

"It will not get that far. The nobles will relent."

"By the cockroaches infesting the City of Kings. Do you seek to make us outcasts among our friends?"

"Impressing others will be your downfall. I always have seen this in you and in your mother."

Jabin sat up at Iyar's dig. "You do not know me. And you certainly did not know my mother. She was one of your victims, taken away before she could defend us. How she would have hated what you're doing, what you've always done."

"I see you." Iyar wiped his face. He appeared sickly, cheeks sagging, eyes meandering. "I see me."

Jabin nearly gasped. He had never seen his father cry, but Jabin reclaimed his outrage and dismissed the tears, which probably served as another of his father's ruses to keep him from doing what he chose. Iyar was the consummate manipulator, the worm that stole life from many green and hearty vines.

"Turn your heart as I have turned mine," Iyar said.

"To Aleph? My brother told me you have landed in that swamp with Aunt Abigail. More foolishness. I warn you, Father. The priests of Livnath will not be your only enemy if you pursue this course tomorrow."

Ezer rested in the shade of several date trees close to the temple ruins. From where he sat, he could hear families eating the morning meal or preparing to sell bread or pottery from their shops. Hunger eluded him. For weeks since the disaster with King Zalmon and the temple sacrifice, he searched for a way to thwart Iyar from purchasing the ruins.

Ezer needed an advantage. If he didn't achieve that, the next time he stood before King Zalmon, the sea horses could take his life. Not just his fingers.

He reached for a date. While the fruit wasn't quite ripe, he crunched the sweet fruit to ease his anxiety momentarily. As he searched the tree for another date, Qatsar ran toward him. The temple priest was reliable since Ezer succeeded Haran as the high priest, although he possessed annoying eccentricities.

"You may recall that I was an aide to the former high priest, Haran."

Ezer dared not mention that Haran was in his dotage beneath the sea with the Water People. A glimpse of Haran among the Water People revolted Ezer because the man sat crumbled near a pile of seaweed, content in a mildewed world. Qatsar never saw Haran beneath the waters, and Ezer wanted to keep it that way.

"You served him well," Ezer said.

"While stacking records that were not destroyed in Haran's home, I found this." Qatsar pulled a tablet from the table. "Haran may have seen the temple fall during his administration, but he created detailed records. They recount the temple tower's construction, repairs, and debts."

Ezer read the tablet. Alongside many projects were names and associated transactions.

"By the night sky," Ezer said. "The temple site is secure."

Jabin brushed past Hulda when he stormed from Iyar's chambers, shaking the pitcher of beer and cups on the platter she carried. She gripped the platter, balancing it as she clucked her tongue. Jabin was the most arrogant of Iyar's three children, although she disliked them all.

Hulda used her shoulder to open the door and found Iyar cross-legged on his couch, holding a heavily embroidered cushion.

"My lord, may I help you?" Hulda hurried to place the platter on a table. Iyar wept, and she didn't know whether to embrace him or slip from the room.

"Do you know why I wanted this cushion?" Iyar asked.

"No, my lord. Naphtali only said it was a gift from the Princess of Edrei."

"The princess pushed the jeweled cushion into my hands when I paid off her debts and halted collectors from storming her palace feasts with indiscreet demands for payment. I saved the princess from being humiliated before the king, a scowling man in ill-fitting garments who hoarded shekels and was her uncle. When I paid the last debt, the princess hugged me until she trembled. I accepted her cushion with a faint smile because I coveted that cushion from the beginning."

"My lord, sunlight peers through your retelling."

"Lies once isolated me in darkness. The company of shadows no longer seduces me." Iyar paused. "But the cushion. My wife owned one just like it. Embroidered by the seamstresses of Edrei. When I first met my wife, she clung to the cushion. She said her mother gave it to her, and it was the most priceless possession she had. I wanted to buy all the cushions I could and surround her with the love she remembered when she caressed the cushion."

Iyar squeezed the cushion before throwing it across the room. "She lied."

"About the cushion?"

"She claimed her mother gave it to her, but that was a lie. The story of her mother allowing her to choose a cushion from the best seamstresses in Edrei was another lie. The love of her life gave her the cushion. A sign of everlasting affection, I suppose. But she married me. She supped on my treasures, but she never let go of that cushion. Day and night, it lay between us. An interloper. A destroyer of my affections. I overheard her sending a message to her love through one of the household slaves, and that is how I discovered the truth. As she dictated her message, my affection for her perished."

"Why keep a cushion like that to pierce you over and over, my lord? It belongs with the foulest of dogs."

"The cushion protected me. Every time I saw it, I stored up more hate. I had emptied myself of love. Unfortunately, and to my regret, my children shared my wounds."

"What happened to the original cushion?"

"I do not know."

"How did she die?"

"She traveled to meet her lover in Edrei but never arrived. A storm. A beast. Who knows who captured her life? I never found her caravan."

"What about her lover?"

"Friends in Edrei said he actually met her en route before she reached Edrei. No one saw him again, either. They perished together. Even in death, her lover possessed what I longed for most."

CHAPTER NINE

GRIEF HAS A NAME

The council-court near the city gate was one of Iyar's favorite buildings in the City of Kings. He had contributed to its elegant architecture, the imported cedar and stone, and felt it was his to enjoy, even though Iyar joined many patrons who wanted their names etched on the pillars as benefactors.

One of Iyar's slaves painted the frescoes, which surrounded members of the council-court in waves of blues, purples, and yellow. Two of his slaves also worked on crews to install the enameled tiles. He was proud of their accomplishments and had publicly credited their success to his selection of them as slaves.

But being in the council-court to defend his business interests dismayed him. Iyar walked around the small crowd, studying the opposition. He knew many of their problems and fears because he had listened; he had divvied shekels to their projects or demanded payment for their debts. In a far corner, where pomegranates adorned a pillar, Jabin, wearing a stern expression, chatted with a scribe Iyar didn't recognize. It didn't matter. Jabin attended the meeting to sit in judgment of his father.

"You long for the temple site land, but you cannot have it, Iyar." Chaggay folded his arms across his broad chest as the nobles, priests, merchants, and scribes in the chamber cheered.

"But I claim it. I will build on a portion of the land," Chaggay said. "In exchange, I will partially underwrite the new foundation for the temple. I will also help pay for the first two platform levels. The priests will pay for the rest."

"Do mud bricks bring in such lucrative revenue? Perhaps I should forego imports and exports for your mud and reeds." Iyar gave a snide grin as several in the crowd laughed in response.

"Construction rises when the population grows," Iyar continued. "People throughout Seth make their home in the City of Kings because of our commerce. And during the spring rains, those rapidly built buildings slide into the street because they are ill made. The mud. Oh, the mud."

"Stop your insults, Iyar," Ezer said. "Chaggay's trade is honest, at least. We know our minds, and we declare before the council-court: deny Lord Iyar's bid. The merchant Chaggay is our choice to buy the temple grounds, under the terms he explained. He's willing to underwrite our rebuilding and in exchange, we will grant him co-ownership."

The council leader stepped forward. "Before we decide, do you have anything else to say, Lord Iyar? You placed your bid first for the temple site. You offered a greater amount. The council-court reserves the right to rule against the priest's request because of their financial vulnerability."

"Only one thing, council leader," Iyar said. "I have the wealth to transform the site into a series of gardens. With the gardens, we could help feed the people of our city. My plan would open the site for everyone. Livnath's priests have found prosperity in their altars within and outside the city walls.

People have accommodated the absence of the temple, and yet their worship continues. My bid helps the entire City of Kings, not just a few. No proceeds will come to my house."

Iyar watched as the council elders gathered to discuss the land bids. He was confident he would get the approval because nothing he said was untrue. Creating a garden would double their food supply because it would complete the palace gardens.

Minutes passed. The council leader finally turned toward the crowd to announce their decision.

Before he could speak, Ezer stepped forward. "Council leader, a word. We also choose Lord Chaggay because of a small matter of the law for Lord Iyar's bid."

"The law? What is illegal about creating a garden?" Iyar asked.

An uncomfortable chill crawled along Iyar's neck and his muscles tensed. He had bribed the council leader and paid off a few debts for other council members to get his bid considered. Why were they reviewing something else Ezer brought to them?

"It is illegal because of a contract you made with our former high priest, Haran," said Ezer, reading from a tablet. "'I, Iyar, will not hold the temple priests in further debt after they repay this loan to me. I will not now, nor ever, demand payment from them or seek to use the land as collateral. I will not try to buy the temple land. I pledge this from today and into perpetuity.'"

"You search in the dust for a contract over ten years old," Iyar said. "It has no significance for the present. Is the council going to allow Livnath's priests to drag in the past on a donkey because they cannot afford a horse to ensure their future?"

"If there is a contract, it has significance," the council leader said. "Ezer. The council would like to view the tablet citing the contract."

The council deliberated for several hours. When they awarded the bid to Chaggay, Iyar sat down on a stool, ignoring the murmurs from Livnath's priests echoing around him and dismissing the mumbled apologies of the council members.

"Do you want to take the matter to King Shammah?" the council leader asked.

My acumen for commerce means nothing, Iyar thought. He should have remembered that detail in his contract with Haran. He should have read the loan tablet fully instead of gloating over the interest he received for the repayment. Presumption had ensnared him.

"No, I need not speak to the king," Iyar said. Resignation sank on his shoulders. "The king would have to uphold the contract, which is legally binding."

Iyar paced the council chambers when everyone left. He had followed in the ruinous steps of the first Iyars. A small decision from his past had crushed future hopes for the kingdom.

When he finally left the council chambers, Iyar chose a whittling path through the City of Kings until he reached his shop. Once inside, he lit an oil lamp, sat at his favorite bench and table where his father restored textiles and chose fabrics for his customers. Slaves had organized the other tablets before returning to their homes hours ago. He was glad they weren't in the shop. The dour, defeated expression he wore would have confused them. Usually, his face and gait boasted profits and success, but this evening he felt like a man of folly.

Cook Levi came for Iyar at the shop when the merchant didn't return home. Silence hung between them when they reached

Iyar's house. Levi didn't start a conversation and only drank beer with Iyar late into the night.

The next morning, Levi commandeered the kitchen, ordering the slaves to prepare Iyar's favorite foods. When Iyar stumbled into the kitchen, he exchanged a glance with Levi over the steaming pots. Iyar nodded, shoulders low, and shuffled to his chambers.

An unexpected message arrived from the palace the following day. Hulda rushed to Iyar's room before knocking hard on the door with her fists.

"My lord, awake. The king summons you."

Iyar yanked the door open, hair sticking on end, tunic stained with wine. He smelled of sweat. Never had Hulda seen him this disheveled. Naphtali warned her he could drink recklessly, and yet he had behaved circumspectly during her employment in his house.

One of the gossipy merchants who brought milk every day told her that the council humiliated Iyar, and Hulda pitied him. He wasn't used to losing or appearing foolish.

She pinched her nose. "My lord, fresh clothes are in your closet. One slave will help you wash. The king is sending a cart for you. You must hurry."

Iyar hung his head; it seemed too heavy to remain steady on his thick neck. "Why does the king want me?"

"Does it matter? He summons you."

The slave came bustling behind her, carrying pails of steaming water. Hulda stood aside.

She knew her face blurred before him. Only her voice mattered. "May I use your words, my lord? By the pigs, by the rats, by the snakes. Hurry."

Shammah handed Iyar a plate of roasted vegetables and watched the merchant pick at the food. The king frowned. The usually impeccably dressed and satisfied merchant looked as if he had spent the night crumpled beneath the feasting tables.

The king overlooked what was unmistakable. "Does the food not please you? Should I order it replaced, Lord Iyar?"

Iyar looked up, shaking his head in apology. "My lord, the palace dishes are the envy of the City of Kings. Please forgive me for being cast down in your presence. Perhaps you can let me know how I can serve you."

"Yes, yes. I thought we could eat first, but no matter." Shammah signaled, and the slaves removed the platters. Then he poured water for Iyar, who accepted the cup absently.

"I heard what happened with the council," Shammah said.

Iyar's expression was so dull that Shammah felt like he pressed through fog.

Shammah softened his voice. "Why not ask for my help?"

"Even you couldn't have broken the law for my sake," Iyar said.

"True. The law curtailed me. The throne has no authority over how the priests use the temple estates. They can erect shrines. As patroness, Livnath, through her followers, has that authority."

Shammah paused. "It is painful to lose."

Iyar coughed and winced as his eyes watered. "It is."

"Despite that, you should have come to me."

"Perhaps. But it does not matter."

"It does matter what you attempted to do. For that, I wanted to express gratitude as your king. I preferred your plan to create gardens to help the poor. Even the Gardens of Destiny can't sustain everyone in the City of Kings. We need more gardens and irrigation systems. Lord Chaggay's construction displays a pattern of poor building. I salute you for suggesting plans far more needed."

Shammah's words prompted Iyar to offer a wan smile, and the small gesture encouraged the king. Perhaps a friendship could begin, or at least after Iyar was more sober.

"Thank you, my lord. I know you think little of me. My reputation as a greedy beast is well known."

"Reputations are long to establish, and their collapse can be sudden and long-lasting. Yours can be restored."

"My sister, Abigail,will rewrite what the storytellers long to say at my burial. A redeemed reputation may only circulate in the City of Kings at my death."

"Ah. A sister worried about your funeral hymns. Far better than mourners paid to cry."

"I am grateful for her."

"Queen Tamiym speaks highly of Lady Abigail. They met at our nuptials and then in the market recently. Your sister mentioned family tablets she wanted to share. After the babes—the midwives prophesy twins—arrive, you and Abigail can make these tablets known to us. I may share some with you. There's a tablet I have in my possession that intrigues me. It's called the *Songs from the Founding.* Perhaps we can discuss it."

Iyar toppled his cup. "I beg forgiveness, my lord. I am clumsy."

Shammah raised an eyebrow but kept speaking as a slave helped Iyar clean up the spill. "The queen and I are constant learners. Knowledge about the ancient families and their descendants would be a welcome diversion."

"You would be interested in our tablets?"

"After the births. Perhaps we can share a meal, a meal you will enjoy, I hope. I am traveling to Nifla for a few days. But I will keep our gathering in mind."

With a wide, cheery smile, Iyar stood up to bow, grateful he didn't stumble on the fringed rug.

"I anticipate our next meeting, King Shammah," Iyar said. "Every blessing as you await your heirs."

The spring thunderstorms accelerated. The roar of the wind hammering the palace walls caused her head to ache. Tamiym sought refuge in the bed, but she couldn't rest because of the twisting pain in her heavy belly. It was the most difficult journey in her life, and the hours of solitude haunted her. The rains stalled Shammah's return from Nifla and marooned her mother in Chaniya, and the midwives expected Tamiym to deliver any day.

Puah brought Tamiym water and caressed her forehead with a damp cloth. "Can I get you anything else, my lady?"

"If you followed Aleph, I would ask you to pray for an end of the rains and a delay in the births. I long for the king and my mother."

"I would like my mother with me if I were bearing young. May I show you the same kindness, my lady."

Tamiym squeezed her hand. "Protect my babes."

With every moan in the wind, the cramps in Tamiym's body intensified. After a few hours, Tamiym shrieked for the midwives.

Shiphrah arrived first and her deep frown signaled that Tamiym's heightened pain meant it was time. She and Puah lifted Tamiym to the birthing stool.

The queen tried to speak to the chief midwife, but fiery pain zipped from Tamiym's chest to knees. She screamed. The raw sound crashed against her rib cage.

To comfort her, Puah gripped Tamiym's shaking shoulders.

"Breathe with me," Shiphrah said.

The older woman's hands deftly cared for Tamiym, and the queen gulped for air, but it wasn't enough. She gasped and writhed, longing for her body to rest, but it convulsed. Its energy focused on bringing new life.

Shiphrah grunted as she worked. Then, slashing over the storm, she shouted, and it seared into Tamiym.

"Again, my lady!" Shiphrah said. "Again, or they will not live."

Seven days after bringing her twins into the world, Tamiym's heart continued to race at their presence. Barrenness and now double fruitfulness for the throne of Seth. Gratitude to Aleph swelled within her. Her son was the lively one with amusement breaking across his face, accompanied by jiggling excitement as he fluttered his arms and legs. Her daughter was softness and warmth, and every time she curled into Tamiym's arms, she cooed and fell asleep. If Tamiym drew away, her daughter seemed to know and stirred, irritated by her mother's absence.

Tamiym couldn't wait to place the babes in Shammah's arms when he returned. By nightfall, he should arrive. She imagined how excited he must have been when the messenger told him their children safely entered the world. Together, they would name them.

She almost reached the wooden crib, when, wooed by the strokes of dawn that swept across the City of Kings, she paused at the balcony, viewing the Gardens of Destiny, its fragrances rising to where she stood, the royal library where she and Shammah toiled, and the city itself that was slowly awakening.

How she became Queen of Seth, the firstborn daughter of a farming couple, a scholar, and a dreamer, escaped her. But here she was, and she had borne beautiful heirs. She turned to the wooden crib and bent over.

She touched their faces. They were stiff and icy. Life had left them hours ago.

"No," she screamed. With tender hands, she touched the small bodies. No wound was on them, no blanket smothered them.

Puah darted into the room. "My lady, what's wrong?"

Tamiym gripped the edges of the crib, her tears dropping onto the babes' faces. "Days. I had days."

Puah picked up the babes in both of her arms, rocking and trying to pat them awake. "They're in a deep sleep, my lady. A fearsome sleep."

"They are dead," Tamiym ground out. "Place them in the crib. I will wait with them until the king returns."

"My lady," Puah protested.

"Put them down and leave my presence. Put them down!"

The midwife placed the babes in the crib and scurried away. Tamiym kneeled beside the crib, dragging her hands across the railing. Once full of life, they would no longer curl in her arms. She couldn't stroke their cheek or wind her finger around their tiny hands. Why was she asleep when they were with her? She should have kept them in bed beside her. It was a mistake to place them in the crib.

She traced the wood, which came from the acacia trees. Her father had spent months building the crib for the babes, a gesture representing a family loving them even before they were born.

A piece of wood creaked in the wind near the chamber door. It must have loosened when the storms roared through the City of Kings, turning the dry months into a basin of water and delaying Shammah's return. Even now, she could hear drops of water dripping. And she started weeping again.

Shiphrah stumbled into the room, dragging her staff. Tamiym glared as the midwife examined her babes.

"Queen Tamiym. I cannot believe this," Shiphrah said.

"Then choose sight," Tamiym shouted. "What was your use if my babes are not with me? All your promises for a delivery led to death. You were there. I was writhing with death while you delivered my children. What killed them? What took them from me?"

"The children were healthy, Queen Tamiym. They slept while you recovered. They were fine when you held them last. I found no sickness of the mouth or foot. The room was not too cold. Or hot. Their bed was not damp."

She hung her head over her staff, the wise midwife, appearing fragile and old. Instead of pity, Tamiym seethed because wisdom hadn't saved her children, and most of all, as their mother, she hadn't protected them.

"My lady, I will ask Livnath."

"Do not speak that name in my presence. Though Aleph has wounded me beyond what I can bear or understand, I do not serve the moon, nor am I besotted by the crone who claims it."

"Forgive me, my queen. But surely the moon goddess has done this. No other wisdom comes to me. The babes were well. Their countenance wasn't sickly."

"Stop. Your words do not undo death. Do not walk from the palace. Run. For my grief has a name, and its name is rage."

CHAPTER TEN

NIGHT WITHOUT DAY

S hammah found the queen by the crib. It was twilight. Tamiym's body was wet and cold from the open window where sheets of rain slammed inside. She hunched into the open window like the mothers who haunted burial grounds, face sallow, unwashed, and garments spattered with mud. After prying her hands from the crib, he wrapped her in blankets, drying her hair and kissing her forehead.

"My dearest one. The solitude of grief ends now. I am here now. I will not leave you."

Tamiym placed a shaking hand on his cheek. "I could not present them to you. I held them and told them about their father. They were beautiful. A girl. Then a boy. I wanted to name them with you."

"We will yet name them, my love. In the presence of Aleph they will not be nameless."

She sighed and wailed. "Shammah, Shammah. Our babes. We lost our babes."

Shammah nearly collapsed when Tamiym's tears wet his cheeks. As he placed Tamiym in bed, she clung to him, digging her nails into his forearms.

"Chayah. It is the name I choose for the girl. Does this please you, my love?"

The wild sorrow shadowing Tamiym's face crushed Shammah's heart. "A lovely name. It is so."

"For the boy, I called him Baruch. Before there was Peleg, there was Baruch. You lost Baruch to sickness one summer. One summer when you were a boy. Then, you lost your father."

Shammah inhaled as he held Tamiym, bemused that she hadn't forgotten his childhood memory. "My beloved, it is so."

Several hours later, Tamiym's soft weeping ended, and she fell asleep. Shammah kneeled to touch the cold faces of their babes. Beautiful, as Tamiym said. Pride and pain lashed him.

"My Lord Aleph, I am without understanding," Shammah said. "Why has this come to my house? How have I displeased you?"

Before dawn, he summoned the palace slaves to remove the children and asked Chazon to prepare them for burial. He returned to the bedchamber where Tamiym slept and burrowed on the couch for a nap. Sunlight warred with darkness in dream after dream. There were mountains. Deserts. Then he heard Tamiym's voice.

"Shammah."

Shaking himself from sleep, Shammah reached for her hand. "What is it, my love?"

"Where are they?"

"Chazon cares for them. They are being prepared for burial. It is time."

"You had no right." Tamiym wailed with her voice and arms. "They belong with me."

Shammah pulled her into his arms. "They will be with you always, my love. Aleph will care for them."

With a groan, she dragged herself from him.

Shammah expected he and Tamiym would cling to each other in sorrow and love. But Tamiym said nothing. For three days, she said nothing. Now they stood at the tomb of their children, and he longed to hold her and for her to hold him. He reached out a hand to Tamiym, but she ignored it.

Shammah dropped his head, then lifted it again to search for Chazon among the mourners. He saw Peleg, Asahel, along with Commanders Mattan and Eitan, who stood with Shammah's mother, Gila. The company that led Seth to victory over the Mikana now suffered as grief tore through Tamiym.

Gila slipped her arm into his and squeezed it, leading Shammah to suspect she observed Tamiym rejecting his hand.

"My beloved son," Gila said.

He kissed her cheek, and Gila returned to stand close to Eitan, whom she had married after the war on a grassy slope of Mount Aleph. The love they shared after deep sadness, war, and advancing years had given Shammah insight about the life he wanted to pursue with Tamiym. But then the twins left them.

Abelia and Sagi wrapped arms around Tamiym, and her brothers awkwardly tried to speak with her, put off by the wordlessness that bound her.

"My lord," Sagi said. "She crept into a cave for refuge, but she will return."

"I long for it," Shammah said. "Without Tamiym, everything is night without day."

Shammah searched for Chazon among the mourners. When the king glimpsed him, the priest rushed toward him.

"I will commit them to Aleph, my lord," Chazon said.

Shammah nodded in relief. Chazon could follow traditional practice and speak words over the babes as the royal morticians interred their bodies, but Shammah and Tamiym didn't have to linger among the royal tombs, numbed by the wails of mourners. Tamiym's slumping shoulders and ashen face plunged him into action.

Tamiym didn't resist Shammah when guided away from the burial grounds. Once they settled inside the covered cart, he hoped his words infused peace.

"Lady Abigail and Naphtali could not reach us in time for the burial rites, my love. They will visit in the coming weeks."

She turned her head aside. Shammah tried again. "I am glad that Queen Gila and Eitan, because of the births, had already traveled here. I am very glad your parents and brothers were here. They are welcome to stay to comfort you."

He reached for her hand again. She jerked away and curled her body away from him. A tiny piece of Shammah pulled from her too.

Hulda pared potatoes, unhurried. Levi, a wiry man who never tired of the smell of onions, left a basket full of them and slapped his slender frame on a stool nearby.

"How long will my pot wait for these potatoes?"

Levi relished pompousness, confident no one fully matched his culinary skills, especially the amateur cooks working in King Shammah's palace. Decades of popular feasts Levi had produced for Iyar were proof.

"You volunteered to help me because our lord was asleep," he said. "Are you asleep?"

Hulda flexed her fingers. "I'm in mourning."

"For whom? You will mourn your position on the streets when Lord Iyar learns of your slothfulness."

"Have you not heard? Have you not seen the women weeping in the streets with Queen Tamiym? She buried her newborn babes today."

"Ah." Levi had heard about the dying babes and rejoiced in their deaths. The loss dampened the people's enthusiasm for Aleph. Aleph of the moody mountain had destroyed the hopes of heirs.

But Levi needn't crow with Hulda. A pragmatic soul, and not devoted to any deity, Hulda viewed mockery as a waste of time. "I didn't know it mattered. I should have. You're a young woman, waiting no doubt for your marriage and birthing years."

"The pain she must feel is beyond my ability to understand. Marriage may not come to me for many years. But when that time arrives, may I not lose a babe during the first years of my union. I can't calculate the grief."

"I will petition Livnath on your behalf." Levi reached around his neck and pulled out a string holding a tiny carved statue of the goddess. The statue was the most cherished of his possessions.

"Livnath grants fertility," Levi said. "My mother dedicated prayers night and day to Livnath until I was born, a firstborn son."

Hulda's face brightened. "Start boiling the water. I will finish soon."

Sweat soaked his back. Tears and tears burned his eyes. For weeks, Shammah had said little unless Peleg was there, and Tamiym uttered no words. Chazon heard their wailings like the mothers who learn of their sons slain in war, or fathers who carried their children's broken bodies after horses or carts trampled them in the streets.

Chazon tightened his hands on the reins. "My Lord Aleph. You ask so much. How can anyone shoulder your desire?"

For two days, under gloomy skies during the day and only a dim cluster of stars at night, Chazon listened to the heavy breathing of his horse until he reached Nifla.

He and Shammah had been here only days before to retrace Shammah's family's history. It was a long overdue trek, but an ill-timed one for a young king and soon-to-be-father. Worry about Tamiym distracted Shammah as the elders urged him to learn more. The visit fulfilled a promise to Nifla's elders, but taxed Shammah. Once the rains came, his anxiety worsened as the downpour delayed their trip home.

Chazon slowed his horse as he reached the city gate. Since it was nightfall, the gates already was closed. Chazon signaled to the watchman for entrance. The watchman opened the gate with a solemn gaze.

"Greetings, priest," the watchman said. "How do the king and queen fare?"

"The unwanted companion of sorrow embraces them," Chazon said.

The priest led his horse through the narrow streets to a corner house, a nondescript structure lit from balcony to ground floor.

The door opened. Abigail stood at the threshold. Chazon had avoided coming to see her for some time. Abigail's hair was as red as he'd ever remembered it, although her face was paler and worn. They both shared the sight of Aleph, and much went unspoken as they stared at each other, soaking in how each had endured. Grief had journeyed from the throne to Nifla.

Naphtali peeked from behind Abigail, curious as he gnawed a piece of bread.

"You've not visited us in a long time," he said.

Naphtali stepped to Abigail's side. "Why are you here? Do you have a message from Queen Tamiym? It was misery to learn about her babes. The old women on the farms say they've lost two or three before one survived. They say it's the way of Livnath to snatch a child. Maybe Aleph is the same way? Maybe the next will live? Lady Tamiym already has lost two."

"Hush, Naphtali," Abigail said. "Treat Chazon, the priest of Aleph, with respect. Burdens weigh on him beyond our comprehension. He does not need our chatter. Most of all, we live here because of him. He has allowed me to stay here these many years. My lord, will you enter?"

The priest leaned into the door. "I dare not. Not until I say it. For two days I rode for this. For two days. I have known no sorrow like this, no regret, no faint of heart, even in battle when soldiers lost their lives, and I nearly lost my own. The will of Aleph smites me. It is done, Abigail, my love. It is done."

"Blessing will come, Chazon," Abigail said. "The evil name and remnant, and the descendants and posterity, will be no more because you placed wheat seeds into the earth."

Chazon sighed before collapsing into her arms.

With a deep breath that whipped through the cave, Lekama threw a boulder into a large pond. Water splashed Mahalath's face, and she wiped it away, knowing pond scum mixed with tears. Her son's outbursts increased her apprehension.

Half-human, half star-born, and petulant boy, Lekama was too young to understand who he was and the dangers that accompanied his strength. Only Mahalath knew, and she was grateful that Zalmon permitted her to keep him away from Qayin's curious overtures and Dahv's lust for vengeance. Livnath and the star-born destined Seth's destruction through Lekama. No one could rush that destiny, however. The boy had much to learn.

From the day she bore him in the cave bordering the Time Sea, she felt the unearthly power of Lekama's father, a Zuzim, ripple through her. She knew she would never bear a child again after Lekama. Bones cracked; bones never healed.

After the birth, Livnath carried mother and babe to Zalmon, spearing the waters until she reached the throne of the Water People. Zalmon felt the honor and the hate. To care for the woman who defied King Shammah, knowing that one day they would take Seth from him, pacified Zalmon.

Lekama stomped from the pond's shore. Mahalath felt the ground vibrate beneath them. "Why can't I be with the others, Mother? I didn't attend your wedding to King Zalmon. I don't go to the feasts. Do you hate me so much? Do I offend your sight?"

His spiky hair crowned his enormous head, and he ran his fingers through the sprouting strands. "Mother, are you ashamed of me?"

"Never, my son." Mahalath crossed her arms across her stomach. "You have much to learn. Control. Self-discipline. You must practice and practice and practice."

Lekama wrapped his arms around her. She thought her ribs would crack and her neck would collapse like a crushed flower stem.

"I don't understand. But I love you, Mother."

He let her go and flexed his shoulders. At nearly four years old, Lekama stood as tall as the willowy Mahalath. Lekama's mortal mind obeyed her like any babe, clamoring for time with his mother, but his body swelled into the strength of the star-born Zuzim, although he was only a small boy in mind.

He tussled with the regal sea horses, rode the turtles that plodded through the caves, and played fetch with the oversized barbels that raced through the waters. But they appeared as toys; Lekama's mind couldn't grasp their strength or his.

One day, mind and body would align. When that happened, they, along with Zalmon and the Water People, would attack Seth. She hoped each of them could wait until it was time.

"My lady, it is good to see your son at last." Qayin stepped from behind a cluster of rocks, and Mahalath felt him slide toward her. Getting caught in the priest's web was an obstacle to avoid in Seth and among the Water People. Self-interest guided him and cost Dahv one of his commanders.

Mahalath believed Qayin drugged Haran at some point so that Ezer could succeed him as the high priest. She had no evidence, and she had delayed dealing with him until she married Zalmon. Now that she was queen of the Water People, she could turn her attention toward him.

Livnath hadn't given her any instructions about Qayin, and Zalmon tolerated him as he did Dahv. Like the sea horses, the two men were useful.

"A rather large boy when he is only a five-year-old babe." Qayin shook his head with sympathy. "Perhaps the stagnant water we're forced to drink fortifies his bones. Or is it the barbel? Maybe sports a wrestler's build because he plays with the sea horses. Whatever the case, his extraordinary growth gave you little time to rock him like a babe in a crib. That must be an endless wound."

Mahalath put a thumb to her mouth and chewed her nail.

Lekama cocked his head at Qayin. "Mother, who is this?"

"A priest of Livnath."

"A son of the moon-mother?" Lekama bounded to Qayin in three steps and picked him up like a wheat stalk. He sputtered in the priest's face like an excited boy. "He's little, Mother."

"Let me go!" Qayin squeaked.

"Release him, Son," Mahalath said. She bowed her head so Qayin couldn't see the satisfaction she felt at seeing the priest dangling in her child's arms.

Lekama plopped the priest on the sand and squatted near him, curious about the unexpected visitor in his cave.

"Did the moon mother instruct you to visit me?" Lekama sounded childish, a mix of man and babe.

Qayin threw back his shoulders. "She sends her regards. Indeed, I'm glad to see you and your fair mother. Tell me about time here. The cave. Does it stay warm and dry enough? What about the pond with the sea horses? Do they ever rest?"

Lekama tousled Qayin's thinning hair at the top of his head. "The sea horses never tire. They fight for breath. They're warriors I should study for military ta-ta—"

"Tactics?"

"Yes, tactics. That's what King Zalmon called them. Tactics."

"Wise words from the king," Qayin said. "Of course, he's your father, now that your mother married him."

"He's not my father!" said Lekama. "He's only a king to me."

Mahalath touched Lekama on the arm. "It's all right, Son."

"My mother married, but I'm not his son," Lekama pouted while he folded his thick forearms across his chest.

"You have not told this beast this? Does he not understand who his father is? At least Zalmon has some mortal blood within him, though he hides it often, preferring fish-like appetites."

Mahalath was calming Lekama when she heard what Qayin called her son. She snapped her body around to face him. "Did you call my son a beast, Qayin?"

Qayin shrugged. "Mahalath, what happened to you was dreadful. That was not love. You father intended you to be the wife of a king, not the secret concubine of a Zuzim. It was a transaction. Like those for buying textiles and vegetables. Sometimes, the gods require that of us. Livnath required it of you. Lekama will be a first-generation offspring of the Zuzim, but a beast forever."

The word "beast" rumbled through Mahalath's mind. She felt a thought grow and heard the goddess whispering to her from the rocks. *Use the power given to you.*

Mahalath gave her son a wild smile, and he grinned as wantonly toward her.

"Mother, your face. It looks different," Lekama said. "I like it very much."

"Lekama, remember that sea turtle we discovered yesterday? The one with the severed leg?"

"Yes, Mother."

"Do you remember how we helped the turtle?"

"Yes, Mother."

"Do that now. For Qayin."

Mahalath turned her back and started walking from the cave. At the cave's opening, she heard Qayin's howls. Mahalath adjusted her stringy hair and sashayed from the cave.

Noonday sun poured over the Gardens of Destiny, along with a sadness that seemed to drench every bloom. While palace slaves tended to the plantings, Shammah watched them distractedly.

"I brought Hulda's rosemary bread. A favorite in our house. But my lord, I have no words of comfort. Every gesture feels awkward."

Iyar bowed. "I offer my sincere friendship and my steadfast allegiance."

Shammah nodded before bending to pull weeds from a cluster of rosebushes. His hand brushed several thorns. The king examined his fingers and sighed.

"During all the years I tended the gardens with the slaves, a thorn never pricked me. It is true. Bees stung me, and I faced other garden ailments. But never a thorn. Every day since our babes' deaths, a thorn has stroked my hands."

Iyar couldn't retrieve a word from his soul. No melodies, longing to be sung, fluttered within him. The merchant felt like anything he said would add pain. So, he stood there, watching the king stare at his fingers and the tiny drops of blood, longing to explain the tablets and the promise they held for the first savior-king who honored Aleph.

"You may ask why touch the rosebushes, then? Because they represent beauty, and their fragrance comforts me. Why Aleph combined beauty, fragrance, and thorns mystifies me, but I will gather roses to me every time."

"As will I, my lord," Iyar said. "As will I."

CHAPTER ELEVEN

SEEING INTO THE REALMS

Adove cooed near the open window in the room where
Chazon slept. Chazon tossed but didn't leave the bed,
undisturbed by the dove's unfaltering, gentle murmurs.

Naphtali watched from his perch in a tree outside the window.
He hoped the dove would awaken the priest so he wouldn't have
to. Lady Abigail asked him to summon Chazon, but the priest,
with his dour expressions and gruff voice, intimidated Naphtali.
He didn't want to talk to him alone.

The dove cooed again, and three more fluttered to the
acacia tree branches where Naphtali observed Chazon. The
priest refused to rise. With a sigh, Naphtali slid down the tree
trunk and leaned into the open window. "Priest of Aleph, arise.
Lady Abigail calls you."

A mumble from the priest, but he refused to rise.

Naphtali scrambled for something else. He remembered
how the priest called Abigail "my love." The two probably
thought Naphtali didn't notice the endearment. But he heard it
and had wondered for the last two days, as the priest slept like a
dead man, how they met and why they had fallen in love.

Affection between Chazon and Abigail puzzled Naphtali because he couldn't imagine how they shared the same air, sunshine, and starlight at the same time. They behaved like roosters matched for a fight or jackals battling for territory. They weren't soft and cooing like the doves, or even like King Shammah, when he pledged to love the beautiful Tamiym. But the affection between Abigail and Chazon wasn't his concern. Knowledge about their love could be useful.

With that observation, Naphtali straightened. "My lord, your love, the dearest and fairest Lady Abigail, seeks your face. Surely you don't prefer slumber to her beauty and conversation and wit."

Before Naphtali could finish, Chazon rushed from the bed and gripped a chunk of Naphtali's locks. It didn't hurt; but Naphtali knew if he twisted to the left, it would.

Chazon's voice was scratchy, like a man who hadn't finished sleeping. "Before you speak, meditate on your speech. I may shred your hair and rip your scalp bare."

"First, Lady Abigail sent me." Naphtali turned awkwardly as Chazon pulled him closer to the window's opening.

"And you called her your love. I heard it," Naphtali said.

Chazon released Naphtali, who tumbled into a rosebush.

"One day, I want to know about your family's house," the priest said. "Where is Lady Abigail?"

"In the scribal school down the path beyond the acacia trees. I can take you there." Naphtali brushed rose petals from his robes and then sucked his thumb, which had scraped against a thorn.

Naphtali waited for the priest to wash and tend to his appearance. When the priest left the house, he bore a frown fixed like a constellation on a foreboding night. Water didn't cleanse the priest's mirthless expressions.

After reaching the flat building, the priest paused. The frown lifted. "They accomplish the will of Aleph here."

"The will of Aleph?" Naphtali asked.

Chazon spun toward him, frowning again.

"Please forgive me, my lord. I forgot. Silence." Naphtali stepped back, head bowed.

Abigail rushed from the building. "Chazon. Come in, come in. Thank you, Naphtali. Why is your head hung low?"

She peered at Chazon with accusation. "Did you cause this glumness? You sleep for two days and harass my apprentice. What am I to do with you?"

"You sound like Iyar," Chazon said.

"I could not. He would say far worse," Abigail said.

"He would say by the pigs and rats or by the cockroaches," Naphtali said. "He has some other phrases, but he rarely says those often. Fury consumes him when he uses those words. I mean, he rages like a desert storm, stunning everyone nearby with his bellowing, the panting and sweating, the stomping, and the arm waving."

"Quiet," Abigail and Chazon said in unison.

Naphtali gulped and rubbed his head. Together, Lady Abigail and Chazon represented an army.

Naphtali wished he could send Chazon back to the City of Kings on one of Gabar's fiery horses because Naphtali feared Chazon might turn Abigail's affections from him.

Inside the building, four boys and three girls sat at long tables covered with fine dust and stacks of carved cuneiform tablets. A pleasant man who nodded his head every time Abigail addressed him fed fresh clay tablets into an oven.

Since arriving in Nifla, Naphtali had worked with Abigail in the building, often organizing tablets and showing the pupils how to write their symbols. Helping Abigail kept him content, especially since he could focus on being in Nifla and not miss Hulda too much.

One child dropped a stylus, and Naphtali scooped it up and touched the boy's shoulder in encouragement. Naphtali felt close to this pupil.

"They are making copies of the genealogy tablets the *malakim* brought to Iyar and Naphtali," Abigail said. "They and their parents are under strict instructions. If they share details about the tablets, they face the wrath of the throne."

"Common wisdom has said there are no tablets dating to the founding," Chazon said. "Only fragments that speak of only a few noble families."

Abigail addressed the children. "Young scholars."

"Yes, Lady Abigail."

"Name your assigned places for our guest, Chazon, the Priest of Aleph. You may have glimpsed him visiting the house. But this is the first time I have brought him to the school. Show him how you have mastered your studies."

"Everlasting," said a tall girl with nut-brown hair and pale-green eyes. "The First Gate. And the birthplace of the Queen Mother, Gila."

"The Forest of Elihu, the Second Gate," said a boy with a voice deeper than his years and youthful chin hair. "Chaniya, the Third Gate," said a girl with the sweetest dimples and freckles. "The birthplace of Queen Tamiym."

"Arba, the Fourth Gate," said a boy who scratched his hair when he spoke to adults. "The birthplace of many prominent nobles and commanders."

"Yaphah, the Sixth Gate," said a small boy who covered his cheeks in embarrassment. "The birthplace of King Aikah . . . and . . ."

The boy shuffled for a few moments. Naphtali stood behind him and pointed to Chazon. The boy smiled and nodded.

"Yaphah, the Sixth Gate, the birthplace of King Aikah and Chazon, the Priest of Aleph."

"The City of Kings, the Seventh Gate," the children said in unison. "Home of King Shammah and Queen Tamiym."

Abigail smiled her praise, and the children giggled before returning to their tablets.

"We will distribute these to the schools throughout Seth," Abigail said. "At each gate of the kingdom. When it is time, when Shammah needs the public confirmation that the City of Kings is the abode of Aleph, and when the Existing One displays power in ways we have never seen, we will decree the truth."

"I stagger at what Aleph plans to do through this school," Chazon said. "The tablets will spread knowledge and provide small tabernacles for our people to learn about the Existing One. But can you trust these children?"

"The tablets from Livnath are safe here in Nifla; Aleph's *malakim* have ensured that. They guard us here," Abigail said. "I have prepared these children since they were much younger. Already, they have shown their gifts from Aleph. When not practicing their writing, they are reading and learning about the world Aleph created. I have promised a pilgrimage."

"A school of prophets and priests," Chazon said.

"Yes."

"Which one will have greater writing duties? There are six children writing, but there are seven gates of the kingdom. Who will work on the tablet designated for the City of Kings?"

"Ah, yes." Abigail whirled toward Naphtali.

Even though the children reciting Seth's gates distracted him, Naphtali still felt like an interloper in the conversation between Abigail and Chazon. He traced a forefinger in the dust on a table and shifted his bony legs left, then right. Then he swiped his nose. Why was Abigail turning her attention to him?

"In time, when Aleph calls Naphtali's name, he will serve as the seventh scribe," Abigail said. "He will copy all three tablets. The third will remove the shadows from many mysteries."

"Naphtali?" Chazon said.

If Abigail's news hadn't flabbergasted him, Naphtali would have frowned in offense. The boy interpreted Chazon's tone to mean, "Who, this flea?"

"My lady," Naphtali said. "You've said nothing of this. I thought I was learning to run your house, to meet your friends in Nifla, and to learn skills for earning wages in the world."

"My intentions have deeper roots. Aleph will call you, and then it will be time for you to assume your position as the seventh scribe."

Chazon shook his head. "Are you sure, Abigail? This boy sat under Iyar's sandal for several years and may not be one to reform. He learned the wrong ways so young. A prophet or a priest of Aleph needs to be disciplined, a rigorous student, and a person of deep and earnest petitions."

"Who were we before Aleph called us? Naphtali already shows skill in the scholarly essentials. Now he needs to walk in his destiny when Aleph calls him."

"Call me?" Naphtali said with a squeak. "What would Aleph say to me?"

"On this we agree, Naphtali," Chazon said. "What would Aleph say to you? Abigail, no doubt he has mingled with the moon worshippers, or worse, with the practitioners of the night arts who give sight for shekels."

"I haven't mingled with anybody," Naphtali said. "My master barely allowed me to visit Hulda."

Abigail's smile became brighter as she gazed at Chazon and Naphtali as if she held mysteries to her heart and longed to share them. "It is not mine to say to Chazon, but when Aleph calls his name, Naphtali will learn the secrets of his family house."

"His house? What house is that?" Chazon asked.

"The house of Iyar is incomplete without Naphtali. Get understanding from Aleph at this moment, my love."

Chazon cocked his head at Naphtali, assessing him for the first time. Naphtali pulled on his hair and shuffled his feet. The children gawked with curiosity. Finally, the priest bowed to Naphtali.

"Naphtali, please forgive my boorishness. My path to Aleph was an uneven one. Had it not been for Aleph's graciousness, I would be unaware of infinite majesty. May you hear the Existing One's voice soon. Already you see into the realms."

"Like at the temple?"

"Remember, only you saw the horses."

Naphtali had wondered why he saw the horses and the failed effort by the moon goddess to manifest her form at the temple. Chazon had given him something to think about later when he was alone.

"Thank you, Priest Chazon. Please forgive me for thinking you weren't much different from my master Iyar once was with me."

Chazon blushed, and Abigail placed a hand on the priest's forearm. "One of Naphtali's gifts is plainspoken sight. We will need it in the future."

"My love, the sight that Aleph grants you peers into the far horizons," Chazon said.

"Does not Aleph's gift to you do the same? You are priest to the king and queen. I am the founder of a school for Aleph's prophets and priests. We are kindred, you and I."

Chazon reached for her hand and kissed it. A few students giggled. "I never knew that Aleph's kindness would include you."

"Friends, then warriors together, and two people in love," Abigail said.

"Three years ago, you could not have told me this."

"Will you tell the king that we plan to marry?"

Chazon's face returned to its usual frown. "Not yet. I will share what burns in our hearts when he and Tamiym can bear it and when grief no longer rolls over them like the Time Sea."

"Does our union remain the path that pleases you?" Abigail asked.

Chazon reached for her hand again. "Like breathing."

Iyar awakened, certain of one visit he had to make. During the late afternoon, he slipped from his house without escort to rummage through the ruins, not knowing what he was searching for or what he would find. Weeks after Iyar lost the bid to Chaggay, workers had measured nothing at the ruins. Survey tools didn't litter the site as they had before. Perhaps the mud construction business wasn't as robust as Chaggay claimed.

As Iyar browsed the tumbled bricks, he glimpsed a mound of earth, almost small enough to be missed.

There.

The thought guided Iyar toward the pile of dirt. His steps felt sluggish, but mercantile instincts he had long practiced kept him going. At least, he thought that was what kept him going. Something valuable lay ahead of him. He was sure of it.

"What are you seeking, Iyar, son of Yissack, son of Iyar?"

Iyar pulled out his dagger. He pivoted on his foot, ready to dive into a fight. The air felt clammy and moist, and he grunted at the smell of stagnant water.

When he saw the creature behind him, Iyar nearly dropped his dagger. Greenish water slicked the creature's blue-black skin with slime, the ears pointy fins, the fish-like pupils flat against the head.

"Who are you?"

"Does it matter when you're about to die?"

The creature reached for Iyar's throat with slender, webbed claws. Iyar felt the coldness bite into his skin like icy seawater.

A fiery sword from chopped through the air and ripped away the claw. The creature squealed and reached for Iyar with the other claw. The sword speared the creature's remaining limb.

When Iyar tried to stab the creature himself, the figure melted into a pool of water before him and clumped into the mud.

"Is this grace from Aleph?" he cried. "After all that has happened?"

Iyar fell to the ground in recognition and in relief. Gabar stood in the ruins with him. The leader of the horsemen who met his caravan in the desert had rescued him.

"My unforgettable apparition."

Gabar extended a hand to him, and Iyar stood, picking up his dagger.

"What was that creature? You are one of the *malakim*, why did you not come sooner?" Iyar asked. "If you do not have wings, perhaps you have chariots. Do the wheels of your chariots roll on the backs of turtles?"

"Cling to patience."

"What would you have me do?"

"Fight for the sacred land. Employ your wealth and wit."

"It did not work. Have you not heard from your desert abode? A tiny oversight cost me, the wealthy Iyar. Hopefully, Chaggay and the temple priests will not discover us here. They will accuse me of trespassing. The City of Kings will run out of wine when Chaggay rejoices during my flogging."

"Aleph knew you before mortal men were born. There is more to do."

"Incompetence soils my hands." Iyar paused. "That creature. It smelled of the sea. Why is that? The City of Kings is days from the sea."

"Allies of Livnath creep from beneath the waters," Gabar said. "As time moves forward, more creatures will appear. You will not avoid the father-serpent, the champion among the Water People for much longer. His spawn and the offspring of the Zuzim attempt to infest Seth."

Iyar rubbed his cheek. He didn't want to think about hovels of dragons and the revolting, human-like creatures staring at him like dying fish. "Wait. I was looking at something before the creature attacked me. I had almost forgotten."

Kneeling, Iyar wiped away the dirt. As he scraped and muttered, Iyar remembered the days when he dove for treasures in bazaars throughout the region, hunting for the obscure and valuable.

"By the pigs and rats." Iyar's thick fingers touched stone. He scrubbed away more soil. It was a memorial. Etched into the stone was the head of the ox, Aleph's symbol of power, strength, and authority. Below the ox head someone had etched the name of his ancestral line: *Iyar.*

The tablets, once again, proved true. Beneath the ruins of Livnath's temple lay the foundation stone, and it belonged to Aleph. The shop owner's words tipped through Iyar's mind like footsteps: *Past, present, and future mingle in the same place.*

"Two that bear witness. The tablets and the stone," Gabar said. "Do not remove the stone. Cover it again with soil. We will guard and conceal it until the time."

"When will 'the time' be? I wait, I fail, I wait. Will I fail again?" Iyar knew he sounded petulant, but he couldn't shed the feeling that the ruins wouldn't return to Aleph, and his family's reputation would never regain its honor.

"We know the purpose, but the timing lies within the heart of Aleph. We wait. Enemies will not steal the foundation stone."

As Gabar spoke, his three desert companions joined him, swords drawn. Iyar wondered if anyone observed them. Then he decided not to worry. He covered the mound with dirt, shaking his head.

"I thought you roamed the desert, Gabar. Is not the City of Kings outside your province?"

"Our voice is heard in the four corners, remember?" Iyar stood and brushed his hands on his robes, shaking his head in surprise. "I can see no one else protecting us sufficiently, especially from water creatures who belong imprisoned in the depths."

"Meditate on the certainty of Aleph," Gabar said. "Many false prophets wander the City of Kings and all of Seth, seducing with their false visions, destroying with vain hopes, and proclaiming lies. Receive the truth introduced to you and come out from among them. Your family history and the catastrophe your ancestors endured should drive you to wisdom."

"The tablets and the foundation stone in these ruins convince me. To have known this before, standing before the council-court would have changed everything. Alas. But of false prophets, I have not listened to them. I have never been that gullible."

Gabar studied him but didn't reply.

CHAPTER TWELVE

BETRAYAL

L evi ducked his tall frame into the squat house where Qatsar paced. Light poured through the large window, but Qatsar's mood was dark. Their meetings often were cordial, but Levi sensed a change in the priest's disposition.

"Do you tarry when I summon you?" Qatsar, a diminutive dust storm, squinted at the taller Levi.

"Lord Iyar's demands are constant. I came as soon as I could. Your message was cryptic."

"Spies are everywhere. A report came to me from Yaphah. King Zalmon tests the ability of the Water People to live outside of the waters. It will take time. But their slowness presents an opportunity for the high priest. He demands our own source of strength. The tablets of Iyar are a strength for the priests of Livnath. Do you understand? Any more hints from the girl you identified?"

Levi grimaced. "Hulda rivals me as a cook. By the snakes crawling the grasses, she'll never know that I think she's better than I am."

"Stop annoying me. If she boils a beet better than you, so be it. Where are the tablets?"

"She's not the one who stole them from where we hid them. I've searched her things. The tablets aren't with her."

"Who then? A thieving rat?"

"Possibly her brother, Naphtali, who once lived in my lord Iyar's house. A few friends, several young women, come to visit her."

"Find out more, you hear me? Find out more."

"I will. I am an elder slave in Lord Iyar's house. And Hulda earns wages like me. Lord Iyar has been generous. Hulda also trusts me."

"But I don't trust you. Find the tablets."

"Have I not been reliable? I'm the donkey you trust."

Qatsar scowled. "Not the description I would attribute to a thief."

"By the pigs, have I stolen from you?"

"Even your reply reveals your sleight of hand. I know you steal from Iyar. It's my reason for using you to spy on Hulda. Her old employer, a friend of mine, couldn't bribe her. But you. You lift your palms at all times."

Levi shrugged. Cooking and stealing were twin companions, his siblings really, since he was a young boy, loping behind his father, who bartered pots and old rags. He knew nothing else and had no reason to seek more. With what he had, he was content and would fight to keep it.

As Levi walked back to Iyar's house, he stopped outside his favorite gambling house, a spacious building with two floors. The owner offered beer and a pistachio pastry Levi failed to replicate for Iyar. The oil lamps, their light peering through the open door, beckoned him.

He patted his tunic. The small sack tied to his waist was empty. While he stood there, annoyed that he didn't have any shekels or anything to barter, the famed gambler, Nasha, spotted him from the balcony.

"Levi! Why hover outside?" Nasha's greeting bordered on a threat.

Levi groaned. He had defeated Nasha many times, but Nasha insisted on playing again and again. Nasha could defeat everyone else in the City of Kings, but Levi. Nasha begged Levi repeatedly to join him at the gambling house. Each time, Levi prayed to Livnath that he wouldn't lose and incur more debts, a weakness that embroiled him with Qatsar. Nasha and Qatsar emulated each other in that way: men who benefited from his constant financial wounds and uncaring that he owed everyone from bakers to cart drivers in the City of Kings.

"You've fed Lord Iyar," Nasha said. "Does he deserve another chunk of bread? I decree, he does not. Flee his supper fires and drink beer with us at the mischief table."

"Perhaps later in the night," Levi said.

Torn, he began walking, shutting out Nasha's ridicule while debating with himself about whether he should go back.

Levi pulled the coins from the jar and tucked them into his tunic. Iyar stashed the coins there for supplies—for farmers who delivered produce, and laborers who repaired a wall or a bench. Only Levi and Hulda could access the jar.

As Hulda watched him, hidden from view, she wondered how many times Levi had stolen from Iyar since the merchant hired him. And had Levi stolen anything else?

An answer to her question came quickly. Levi pulled fresh bread from the oven and fruit and meat from the table and wrapped it in cloth, along with one of Iyar's prized utensils and plates. Levi bundled the items into the cloth and left the kitchen.

Hulda sat on the stool and raked her tresses with her fingers. She never expected Levi to violate Lord Iyar's trust. Only hours ago, they had baked Iyar's bread and laughed about the strange scenes they had witnessed in the City of Kings and how Iyar, despite his ornery sense of privilege, had placed them in positions of respect and stability. They could earn their own money, buy their own belongings, and, if they wanted, purchase their own quarters.

"Hulda. Where are you?" Iyar's voice boomed into Hulda's thoughts. He panted, his sandals slapping the floor.

"Hulda. Will you not answer?"

"Right here, my lord. How may I help you?"

"A letter. A letter to my sister. Alert her. I am coming to Nifla. You cannot come this time. I need you here with Levi. You and Levi can tend to my affairs. Where is he? I see the fresh bread. Where is the rest of the meal? Why is no one cooking?"

"Levi cannot remain in your household, my lord."

"And why is that? Do I detect jealousy? Do you think I prefer his dainties to yours? Your soups are the best, not his. Do my words ease your fretting?"

"He steals from you. Coins, food, utensils."

Iyar wrinkled his forehead and took a long breath. "What are you saying?"

"He's a thief. I need to check the rest of your quarters to see whether he's taken anything else."

Iyar shook his head. "I have withheld nothing from him but my children's inheritance."

Hulda had never seen Iyar downcast about anyone in his house. It unnerved her that his breathing sped up again as he paced around the kitchen.

"I've wondered why we're always short on money for supplies and small labor," Hulda said. "Once, I thought it was because of high fees. Levi told me that. It wasn't true."

She bit her lip. "Naphtali and I stole bread to survive for months before the shopkeeper found us. But I didn't recognize a thief tended a kitchen fire with me. Foolish, foolish."

She drove her fingers deeper into her hair, tangling her curls. "My lord, what do you want me to do? Should I alert the magistrate?"

"No, no, no," Iyar said. He waved his hand. "I will see to it."

Levi had defeated Nasha for the third time in the gambling house when Iyar found him. The cook squatted on the floor, moving dice on a small table to the guffaws of his friends.

"One more chance on the mischief table," Levi said.

Iyar noticed Levi laughed with a cheerful pig's joy, thrilled to roll one more time in mud thick and foul. Iyar remembered playing in this gambling house, drunk after his wife left him. This house never brought him comfort, but he ran to it like an overflowing well.

Levi tossed his dice, brushing Iyar's sandal. Only then did Levi notice Iyar, accompanied by the magistrate and two aides.

Stumbling to stand, Levi jerked his neck around, eyes red, tongue sliding over his lips. Beer had entertained him for hours.

"Lord Iyar, what brings you to this house? Is all well? Did Hulda forget to prepare the vegetables in case you needed them? If you permit me, I'll beat her. I prepared instructions. Beets, radishes, and turnips. The priests said the mixture would ease aches in the stomach. Why does Hulda rebel? I can recruit others for service more faithful than her."

"By the mice creeping in the straw, Levi," Iyar said.

The merchant kicked clumps of dirt, scattering the other gamblers, including Nasha, who skulked outside. "Did you ever go lacking in my household?"

Levi came to Iyar with a lopsided walk. "I'll recruit that new cook, my lord, and take the magistrates with me to thrash Hulda after this last round. The mischief table is a beautiful woman. I must tend to her."

Levi fell onto the table. "Her embrace is so sweet, my lord."

"You will never steal from me again," Iyar said. "I did not choose this for you. But in forced labor, you will remember the goodness shown to you in my house. May you shiver in the rainy seasons and cry for cold winds during the heat."

Tamiym couldn't bear the pain on Shammah's face. By excusing herself from the courtyard where Shammah waited for Peleg to arrive for his nightly visit, the two men could swap sailor stories to numb their pain about the lost babes.

They already had done this for days, leaving Tamiym feeling more isolated. She had sent her parents to Chaniya and rebuffed Gila's invitation to visit Yaphah. The only solace Tamiym sought was in restless solitude or in agitated sleep.

Once in bed, Tamiym couldn't escape the sight of her dead children and Shammah's lusterless face. She flung on a hooded robe and waved away her bodyguards.

She broke into a light run in the long hall. She stopped at a sealed door. She longed for the key that Shammah kept somewhere else in the palace. Inside the locked chamber stood the cribs carved by her father. Acacia wood, engraved with giraffes, egrets, and gazelles, coated with sorrow.

Tamiym placed her hands on the door. Many times, since the babes' deaths, she had paused at this door only to rush back to her bed, attacked by grief.

This time, when tears fell, she moved from the door, tipping past the courtyard where Shammah sat by lamplight, waiting for Peleg. Tamiym resisted an impulse to join Shammah and slipped into the Gardens of Destiny, hoping a walk would make her drowsy.

The wind was cool, driving her to weep in memory of her babes' lifeless skin. The bodies of her children, once warm and living, lay cold and dead in their tomb. Her babes needed her to protect and love them.

She huddled on a bench near the Ten Pillars where palace artisans etched every king's name. Tears fell on her cheeks when she read:

SHAMMAH

CALLED BY ALEPH

TO BE KING

Grief clung to the heels of her joy. Aleph, the source of all power, had opened her womb and stolen its fruit. Aleph had gathered to himself the heirs of the only Lord of the Seven Gates who called the Existing One beloved.

Tamiym shivered, her body aching from the hard shaking of her bones.

Tamiym.

Reeling from hearing her name, Tamiym gripped her trembling elbows. It was Aleph, reaching for the coldness within her, the coldness she refused to let go. She wanted to crawl into the tomb, cling to her children, and breathe life into them.

Tamiym.

In a vision, an olive tree sprang from within the Gardens of Destiny, tall, radiant, and full of light. Its branches expanded before her, and oil seeped from its leaves.

Tamiym.

Then the coldness within her fled.

CHAPTER THIRTEEN

THE CALLING

"Sister, have we followed the right path?" Iyar held a basket while Abigail plucked herbs along with radishes and lettuce. She focused on the plantings. He felt his heart beat faster. Three weeks had passed since Iyar ordered Levi to the workhouse. Punishing the cook meant redirecting his household and sleeping less because Iyar worried about who lurked in a pantry or a bedchamber to betray him.

The day was bright, and the sun lit the strands of Abigail's auburn hair as she reproached him with a silent gaze for appearing overwhelmed.

He lifted a hand. "No platitudes from Aleph. They leave me impoverished and wanting when there's an abundance of sorrow. The Existing One left our father Yissack dead on the streets of the City of Kings, robbed by the ungrateful children he helped. He and his four horsemen led me to pursue foolishness at the temple ruins. He killed the babes of King Shammah. And did not Aleph instigate the thievery Levi committed in my house?"

"The Existing One isn't a murderer or an instigator. And do you see me wanting, Brother? What Naphtali and I have will expand because of your storehouses."

"Why would I share any of my wealth with you and that worthless slave and his equally worthless sister? It is only because of you I have not had Naphtali thrashed in the streets."

"Because you have sight like I do. I also know you do not speak truly. Without Hulda, distress would overtake you after losing Levi, who've you trusted for years. You also know who Naphtali and Hulda really are. You will not say it, but you suspect it. You know who your children are, and you know we must withhold the tablets from the king. For a time."

"You swim in riddles."

"Riddles you understand."

Head bowed, he tore the leaves from a poppy plant. Of course, he knew what Abigail meant. Lying ahead of them were battles, intense and many. It was no accident that Naphtali and Hulda served him, and from Levi's confession, he not only had learned the full conspiracy led by the high priest, including the attempted poisoning, but he finally grasped how he couldn't treat the ancient tablets carelessly. Thankfully, Abigail and Chazon stored them safely in Nifla.

Abigail pushed on. "Leave that plant alone."

"I did not intend what you are thinking."

"Do not present the invitation to someone else," Abigail said. "Uproot them. I will send someone to do it."

"I have slaves who can do that."

"Workers." Abigail adjusted her basket.

"Slaves by title. They expect me to feed them wages."

"As they should," Abigail said.

"They will lead me to ruin."

"Your children brag now about your prosperity."

"I failed to leash them," Iyar said.

"Now is the time to restore our house, Brother. There can be no distractions from our purpose. You and I must bring the reckoning our ancestors could not."

"Like olive trees." Iyar cast a glance at his olive grove, only footsteps away. The grove was one reason he loved the home.

"Do you remember the song?"

"It is ever with me." He cleared his throat and sang, hoping the melody would overshadow his pensiveness about what was to come:

> *Love captured me at dawn,*
> *Filled me with joy at noon,*
> *Carried me away at sunset.*
> *Protected me beneath the midnight stars.*
> *May I know your affection always*
> *Because your love crosses seven hills,*
> *Never forgetting*
> *An olive tree blooms forever for love for me.*

Abigail brought up the song again when they returned to the courtyard with the plantings and watched the slaves sort them, filling the air with the fragrance of vegetables and herbs.

"I loved the nights when you sang after father's stories. I have missed your song, Iyar."

"Do you know more about the hymn? It is a part of me, like a rib or an arm. Mother sang it so often."

"Father's tales of pirates and thieves intrigued you. According to Father, this was the song Hannah, the first wife of Iyar, sang to their children from the time they were babes. They sang it over Iyar's body after the elders murdered him."

"I dislike the song now," Iyar said. "Mourning hymns repulse me."

"Brother, reconsider," Abigail said. "Some scholars think the song came after the Deluge when a dove clutched an olive leaf in her beak at evening as the waters receded. Others, especially the scholars here in Nifla, think the song is a hymn Aleph sung over Seth, and the first followers of the Existing One. It is a vow, a covenant, and a promise whenever we sing it."

"Then I will not sing again," Iyar said. "Do you not see me drowning in disappointment?"

"A promise is not a disappointment. It is a marker for expectation, a vow that soars beyond the horizons."

"I cannot vow anything, especially without knowing that I am doing it."

"This type of vow you can't keep. Only Aleph can."

A young woman with tousled black hair and a tentative smile scurried toward them, wiping wet hands on her rumpled tunic. "My lord Iyar, I would not disturb you, but Cook Hulda sent me. You have a guest. She came through the kitchen. Cook Hulda sent me after speaking with her. She says the woman must see you."

"Who is this woman?" Iyar asked.

"She refused to give her name but gave us this at the door," the young woman said.

A second slave, a boy who Iyar often assigned to meet guests because of his jovial temperament, joined them and handed a lyre to Iyar. The merchant thumbed its strings and stroked the neck of the instrument.

Abigail frowned. "Are you bewitched? Who is this visitor?"

"Send her to me," Iyar said.

When Raushanna entered, the slave accompanied her, cupping her elbow. She was plumper, though no less beautiful. Her stomach was round as fruit. Iyar felt his heart plunge.

Immediately, Iyar remembered their last performance together. By lamplight, shortly before they greeted their audience, Raushanna stopped practicing and sat beside him. Smoky cinnamon fragrance wafted from her robes as she scooted close beside him on the couch.

Desire screamed for him to slip his arms around her while discipline drove him to focus on the song they planned to perform, a hymn about a soldier dreading life after war. Raushanna selected the hymn, agitating him because it was a traditional one he had often heard on his trade routes. The melody slung the verses like swilling beer, mocking the warrior's sorrow.

He thumbed the tablet in his hand inscribed with the hymn. "Perhaps we should revise the song? It does not capture the warrior's loss after losing so many friends on the battlefield. Maybe if I sing the hymn more slowly, it will sound more forlorn? When I sing the passage, 'he remembered men, lying beneath their shields, their breath no more,' I could sing that in a lower tone, and the lyre could trail alongside me."

Raushanna pulled back her dark hair to reveal glowing brown eyes. "Songs dance in the waters within you, Iyar. Why do you flee from them?"

"Wounds. Time hides the gashes, but they are there."

"You use your money to cloak the past, to cover what's naked and ugly. I've seen men like you, dipping into the seas of lives not their own, and shunning the waters where they truly belong. I hear their footsteps behind me on my tavern rounds. Eager they are to sail to a place that already lies within their hearts."

Annoyed, Iyar moved away from Raushanna and the thick cinnamon fragrance. "By the pigs and rats. What are your thoughts about the hymn?"

Raushanna pressed her tapered hands to his chest. "Some of them crash on the shore. Some sail on to the horizon, survive the storms, and reach land. I wish that for you. The music within you eases your heart sickness and casts it away."

"No, no, no. Your music heals me." Iyar put his hand on hers. "I am the twelfth string on your lyre."

Turning from him, Raushanna picked up her instrument. "Don't deny the gifts the gods have given. Even in Midvar, our goddess favors you."

Iyar grunted, caring less about the goddess and more about Raushanna's fitful turns of affection. He was a ship sinking in her skittish seas, and that set the perfect mood to sing Raushanna's hymn about that soldier, cast down and bereft of hope.

Now Raushanna, a phantom rising from his memories, stood in his house. The slave guided her to Iyar and stepped back. Iyar knew he should send the two wide-eyed slaves away, but Raushanna with black tresses lined with grey waves, a flowing tunic as red as the palace roses, and a low, hoarse voice were too intriguing. For once, Iyar allowed his household staff to indulge their curiosity as he tried to satisfy his own.

"I had nowhere else to go." Raushanna clasped her belly with both hands.

Iyar plucked a few strings on the lyre before playing a morose melody. "I would have stayed in Midvar had you taught me to play."

"You mastered the lyre," Raushanna said. "Without me."

"You saw nothing. Understood nothing. Felt nothing." Iyar tossed the words like mud bricks.

Abigail stood. "My lady, please forgive my brother's rudeness. Iyar, please explain."

Iyar almost laughed. Abigail's frustration was comical; she didn't understand how Raushanna could raze a man's soul.

"How long has it been? Over two years? No word. No song," Iyar said. "And now you come to me. Plump with child. Was it the priest?"

"Do you not see that I came to you, to you alone?"

Raushanna's voice remained as lyrical as her instrument, and Iyar walled his heart from the sound.

"I presume you chose not to live in the streets after the priest abandoned you. I would have come begging if I had a rich friend like me," Iyar said.

Abigail placed herself between Iyar and Raushanna. "Brother. Your unkindness shames me."

Raushanna stepped around Abigail to face Iyar, unconcerned by Iyar's words and childish scowl. "Before enemies murdered the priest, he told me to find you. He said you alone would keep me safe."

"My companions do not include Midvar priests. What would your priest know about me?"

"His father knew Lord Yissack."

Abigail frowned. "What root of mayhem is this? My father never traveled to Midvar during his lifetime. He only traded with Midvar merchants who traveled to the City of Kings."

"They found each other through friends in trade," Raushanna said. "They also knew the ancient story about what happened after the Deluge, which sealed their friendship covenant."

"Misbegotten lore," Iyar said. "Why did not your priest introduce himself to me and search for the house where I lodged? Did debts prohibit him from caring for you and his child? Murder was a convenience."

Abigail nudged Iyar. "Revenge curls your tongue."

"An assassin killed the priest," Raushanna said. "Anticipating they might murder him in Midvar, he sent me here. He chose not to reach out to you openly. Every desert route hails your name."

"Insolence roams like the four winds," Abigail said.

"Ah, but I am known, Sister," Iyar said.

He stroked the lyre again. "Why would anyone want to kill your priest, Raushanna? From what I remember, you loved a lackluster and clumsy man."

"Cruel words you still possess," Raushanna said. "He hailed from an ancient house. Enemies longed for his goods and land."

"Then I assume you have payment for a room in my house." Iyar lifted a hand and motioned to a slave. "Find the lady a bedchamber, one of the larger ones where she can deliver her babe when it is time."

The slave who still rubbed her hands on the tunic nodded. "My lord, the bedchamber overlooking the olive trees?"

"A thoughtful choice," Iyar said. "The trees have been here since the beginning."

"The beginning," Raushanna said. "A grove of olive trees as first sight for my child? My babe stirs with pleasure."

"Have you written a hymn for the birth?" Iyar asked.

"Not yet. But living in your house will be the perfect place for my song."

Abigail trailed Raushanna as the nervous slave led them to the chamber overlooking the olive trees. Abigail loved the room, inviting with its two large windows where starlight settled like a garment, the haven of her yearnings when she stayed here years ago.

Estrangement hadn't separated them. Mother was still alive. Fire hadn't destroyed their ancestral home. They were young adults. Expectant about the destinies that lay before them. She dreamed of an apothecary or a school. Eli forsook his family's wealth to work on a farm as an apprentice. Iyar chatted endlessly about reviving their father's textile business.

When Iyar bought the house, the ancient trees intrigued him as they did her. The braided trunks and the branches bore some of the best olives in the City of Kings, and the histories said the trees stood as silent watchers of Seth's founding, when the people chose the first king, and they renamed the plain the City of Kings instead of Ariel.

Abigail glanced at the table and stool, where she once read tablets about planting, irrigation practices, and herbs. When she tired of that, she recited poetry and the writings of Aleph's priests. Raushanna would sit in her place now.

Raushanna leaned on a window ledge and let a wide smile break across her face. "They produce rich oil."

"How do you know that?" Abigail's voice rose.

"From stories told by the priest." Raushanna shrugged. "He heard this from your father."

"This is not our ancestral home. My father never knew this place."

Raushanna turned from the window, hand to her chest in apology. "My lady, I confused times and seasons. The priest mentioned fourteen olive trees. I'm not as skilled in the retelling. Memory intertwines with music. Perhaps the priest distilled stories from your father. I can't say. The priest's words covered me like warm oil. Because of him, I've longed to come to the City of Kings."

As Raushanna turned to the window, Abigail knotted her fingers behind her back, a habit she gleaned from Chazon, and one that framed her thoughts in a perceivable order. Raushanna traveled from Midvar to deliver her babe in the care of Iyar. Maybe Iyar's cruel words revealed more pragmatism than unkindness. The house of Iyar offered every delicacy and support needed by a woman with child.

Abigail tightened her fingers. If Chazon were beside her at this moment, she was certain he would express the same questions surging within her mind. Perhaps he would snort in disbelief. Abigail smiled. A snort from her lips, no. More questions to pursue, yes. Raushanna lied, but why evade the truth? And why would olive trees matter to a lute player from Midvar whose sleepy gaze seduced her brother to behave like scattered grains of salt?

"You flatter all of Seth," Abigail said.

"Do I? My thoughts are not so empty, I assure you. My admiration is sincere. The priest believed in healing and thought the trees carried remedies from the beginning of time. Your father must have told him."

"My loss not to have not met this priest."

"He was wise, my lady. Very wise."

While Raushanna lifted her body onto the bed with a gleeful sigh, Abigail remembered the musings and prayers she once poured out in this chamber. Only Aleph could recount her many petitions.

The window curtain fluttered as Raushanna snuggled a pillow. "The breeze flowing through this room reaches perfection."

An icy gust, not a warm breeze, stung Abigail's cheeks. She hugged her shoulders, unable to stop shivering, and contemplated what nightmares Raushanna would drag into Iyar's house.

Carrying two baskets, Hulda couldn't see far ahead of her as she navigated to Iyar's house. Only a few months ago, Levi would have helped her, debating her about the best pots and produce, and making sure he carried most of the baskets. She sniffled. She would miss the thief.

A few figs slipped from the fullest basket. As she reached for them, a stout man wrapped his arms behind her and swung her onto a narrow back street.

Hulda dropped both baskets and screamed. She chomped into the man's arm and kicked him repeatedly. "Let me go, you street rat. Help! Help!"

Her assailant twisted her arm and covered her mouth. "Scream again and watch me nip your throat."

A shorter man stepped up to them from the shadows.

"Hold her still," the man said. "Where are the tablets? Does your brother hide them?"

Hulda writhed again, but the man who held her wouldn't loosen his hold.

"Let her speak," the man said.

The assailant removed his hand from her mouth and gripped her arm.

"To tell you what, street rat? Let me go," Hulda said.

The shorter man slapped Hulda. With blood dripping from her lips, she grinned. "You prefer another name than street rat, don't you? Flee the dark corners, then."

He punched her. Then he aimed to slap her again as Iyar stepped between them.

Iyar twisted the man's arms until the bones cracked. A slave from Iyar's house grabbed Hulda's assailant in a stranglehold until the man released her. Hulda gulped for air with a surprised expression.

"My lord."

Iyar helped Hulda to stand and wiped her face with his sash. "Hulda?"

"Address the street rat," she said. "I will survive his childish blows."

"Qatsar," Iyar said. "You strike my friend and defile her person? And you cost me my meal tonight? Join Levi in the workhouse."

Qatsar slumped on the street, wailing. "You broke my arms. I know you did. The high priest will punish you."

"He will not," Iyar said. "Ezer does not want his dark deeds exposed, for they will reveal the truth the tablets reveal. The truth he wants to hide."

Qatsar moaned again. "I'll never hold a cup again."

"You will. I will send a physician," Iyar said. "After your healing, you and your accomplice will never return to the City of Kings."

Once Iyar confirmed Hulda had received the care she needed, he instructed the slave known for her healings to leave.

"Sleep, brave Hulda." Iyar began closing the chamber door.

"My lord," Hulda said.

Iyar frowned. "Did not the girl nurse your wounds sufficiently?"

"How did you know to come and find me?"

"The *malakim* led me to you."

"The *malakim*? What are they?"

Iyar gave her a half-smile. "Naphtali has not explained this to you?"

Hulda pouted. "He has not."

"On your next visit, chide him for his forgetfulness."

"When *you* visit him, my lord. He forgives and remembers what you taught him."

"May he only remember what betters him."

"Naphtali makes me smile," Hulda said with a welcoming smile of her own. "He will cheer you too."

"Perhaps," Iyar said. "But the gnarled branches of my life may darken the light Naphtali supplies for everyone."

While a slave held an oil lamp in the twilight, Iyar examined several trees in his olive grove. Disease or insects hadn't harmed them, but the dark meditations that roiled within him caused him to worry about the trees. He counted on producing oil if his textile shop failed.

Raushanna's unexpected arrival probably stirred his anxiety about his property, his belongings, his heart. Her beauty captivated; her presence tainted. She was no more his now than she was in Midvar.

As if summoned, Raushanna stood near him in the twilight. "My lord, why walk alone?"

"Why are you not sleeping? Mother and babe need rest."

Raushanna stepped around several trees. "Like elders, these trees speak."

"Then listen in the day. To your chambers, Raushanna."

"Your words reprove like a father, but fear lies behind them. Why do you fear me, Iyar?"

Iyar took the oil lamp from the slave and shooed him away. "You may leave."

Raushanna giggled as the slave left, cocked her head, and danced like a young girl.

"It's only me, Iyar."

"Go to bed."

Humming, she bowed and left him.

Raushanna's humming dominated his thoughts even an hour later as Iyar finished inspecting the olive trees. He wanted the humming to stop and instead, it became a throbbing, hissing sound.

"By the mice. What is that?"

The hissing grew louder. Angrier. In moments, a water creature snaked around Iyar. Odors from the sea encircled the creature, but no water dripped from its body. Unlike the creature that attacked him at the temple ruins, this one seemed to have adapted to dry ground.

Iyar pulled out his dagger. "You trespass."

The creature stepped closer with an outstretched hand. Iyar swiped at the hand.

"You can't strike me and hold that oil lamp, can you?"

The creature snapped forward as Iyar plunged his dagger into the creature's chest. The creature lunged forward again. Iyar dropped the oil lamp. Oil oozed on the ground.

With a foul heave, the creature blew over the oil, causing curling, red-orange flames.

"We know what you fear," the creature said.

Iyar stabbed the creature again. Once the merchant felled the creature, Iyar realized several creatures surrounded him in the grove.

"Help! Someone, help me!" Iyar yelled.

Several slaves ran to the grove, but the creatures slapped and thrust them away.

Flames chewed at an olive tree. "Stop them, stop them!" Iyar said.

A creature broke off a branch and jabbed it into Iyar's ribs. "Where are the tablets?"

"Get off me, foulness!"

The creature dug into Iyar again and pierced Iyar's skin.

"Lord Aleph, I ask for the *malakim*!" Iyar began coughing from the smoke.

Winds stormed through the grove. The creatures sprinted away, but the winds seized them and doused the fire. Relieved, Iyar and his slaves collapsed to the ground. Iyar had worried that fire would destroy the grove; the ground crackled with dryness because the rains hadn't arrived.

"Thank you, Mighty Aleph," Iyar said.

In the morning, when he examined the grove for damage, he couldn't find signs of flames.

When Gabar joined him, suddenly appearing, without steed, companions, or winds, Iyar smiled.

"I thank you, Gabar," Iyar said.

"I heed the summons of Aleph," Gabar said. "You brought joy to the heavens by calling out to the Existing One for help."

"Who but Aleph and his *malakim* can stop these sea creatures?"

"The boiling thirst in them for the tablets will only increase. I will help you grow in strength."

Peleg sloshed down a cup of beer. He had already had too many. Shammah and Tamiym's losses were his own, and with each beer cup, he longed for their sorrowful faces to flee his thoughts. Staring at his cup, he felt hot. Then cold. After that, sick.

"Your answers aren't in the dregs." The grizzled tavern owner shoved another overflowing beer cup toward Peleg.

Peleg gulped the beer and held the cup high for another. "Then why grant me my fateful desire?"

The tavern poured the draught without losing a drop. "There's a man outside who told me to. You're the king's man. Your place near the throne fits the interests of a special set of people."

"By the cockroaches in this place, I bet it does. Who's talking to you? I'll chop the ruffian into three pieces. Maybe four," Peleg said.

He lifted his cup for more beer. Once the tavern keeper filled it, Peleg stumbled from his stool.

Balancing the cup in shaking hands, Peleg called out: "My dagger to your throat, you troublemaker to the king!"

Peleg bumped into a slim man wearing a hooded cloak. "Are you the ruffian I intend to cut up for insolence?"

"Unless you follow my instructions, the throat of your son will feel the dagger, which would be a pity. Only today he learned of his father. A thief turned sailor, a sailor turned king's confidante."

"I have no children, pig."

"You would think that, but you left her in that fire, did you not? Is not that why you fled to the sea? Your thievery was nothing compared with your cowardice."

Peleg tossed his cup. Now, along with the tormented faces of Shammah and Tamiym, he remembered the tortures caused by that fire. The woman was only eighteen years old, a haunting figure who trailed Peleg's thoughts from port to port. When he remembered her screams, they rolled over him unbidden, and his hands trembled.

"Who are you? Where is she?"

"I am the one who owns you."

The man brushed Peleg's throat with his dagger. "Everything the throne does, I want it told to me. If you refuse, I will expose your cowardice. Livnath will hound you from moon to moon. They will both die. Mother and son."

CHAPTER FOURTEEN

SEA OF JOY

Tamiym nestled in the crook of Shammah's arm, her breath spilling onto his chest as the last strokes of sunlight turned a few gray strands of her hair to gold, the almond oil in her braids filling his nostrils. She energized his senses by murmuring his name in the morning and soothing him at night when stroking his cheek, his queen, his inspiring scholar, his gift from Aleph, his mystery. Day by day, his doubts grew darker, however. He yearned for her thoughts, the part she walled off from him. She clung to him this evening, but something—or someone—stepped between them.

Tamiym shifted and stirred sluggishly. Shammah was glad her slumber persisted so he could stare ahead at the Ten Pillars. Shammah never wanted to be the man Aikah was, full of rage and misguided worship for Livnath, and yet his anger burned as his suspicions about Tamiym grew.

His wife was awake. She slid from his arm to face him. Behind her, as twilight fell, palace slaves lit oil lamps around the pillars. The light glowed on her face.

"My love?" He forced the gruffness in his voice to yield to gentleness. "Did you rest enough?"

"You let me oversleep."

"You needed it."

She paused and placed a hand on his chest. "What were you thinking? Moments ago? At first your breaths came rapidly. Like you were running. Then they slowed."

"You were not really asleep, then."

"What were you thinking?"

"My thoughts wander where they should not."

"Tell me."

He inhaled, knowing he needed to explain because she would needle him until he did.

"Tell me." She lifted a lock of his braided hair from his jaw.

He lifted a forefinger toward the Ten Pillars. "What words would Aikah give? What words would he offer about my kingship?"

"He would not fully understand, but he knew the throne was yours. Never Dahv's. Dahv was Aikah's son, the heat of his heart, a warrior, but not the chosen heir. Aleph used Aikah, despite his flaws, to bring you to this place. Why doubt now? You have held the throne for twelve years."

Sharp edges of suspicion taunted him. Shammah didn't trust himself to speak.

Tamiym didn't wait for him to reply. "New hope will come to you, my love. I promise."

His mind slipped back into a normal rhythm. Peleg often told him how she comforted him. Thinking about the sailor, Shammah chose that moment to change the subject.

"Have you seen Peleg lately? Has he been to the library?"

"He toured with me the other day. You have not seen him?"

"Left alone, I may have to rescue him from a bad wager."

"My love, perhaps you view him with old eyes. The nobles who enjoy his company have invited him to their feasts, hunting gatherings, and caravans. Peleg the sailor is Peleg the popular."

"Once a man no one trusted with their bag of shekels."

"I know the friendship you have."

Tamiym's words softened Shammah. "I will send for him."

"I must leave you, my love."

Shammah frowned. "Not for long, I assume. A queen belongs near the king."

"I will pilgrimage to Aleph."

Sadness pressed against Shammah's chest. They always traveled to the mountain together. Did the rift he suspected between them mean she wanted them to no longer share their love of Aleph?

"I cannot conceal my sadness for we do not pilgrimage together," he said.

She placed a hand on his cheek. "I must travel in solitude, but it does not release me from the shores of our love."

He drew back from her. "The Shamgar will accompany you. Your bodyguards are untried in the ways of Aleph. May the Shamgar serve as the lamps that will light your return to me."

When Tamiym saw the cliffs of Mount Aleph, she wept. As the sun sank in the west, pilgrims had planted themselves in piles, lighting fires, singing hymns and rocking their drowsy infants in what had become known as the fruitful garden in the west. Aroma from the fires stirred Tamiym's longing to sit with them and share dry bread and a broth. She patted her murmuring stomach, and, in the same instant, moaned when she noticed an herbalist pounding bark. Tamiym's right heel ached with a blister. Bark could ease the pain if the herbalist examined her foot. She couldn't stop, though. Clouds would soon reveal the moon.

In a small grove of oak trees, clusters of men and women wandered at the edge of the pilgrims' fires. Gossips in the City of Kings often murmured within Tamiym's earshot when in the royal library or in the market that the priests of Livnath slipped among Aleph's worshippers. Tamiym didn't need mutterings to confirm what she already knew. Livnath's priests feigned loyalty to Aleph, just as they offered false fidelity to Shammah, along with endless and insipid proverbs for his barren queen.

She suspected their seduction as she scanned the small grove: in the tossing eyes of a square-faced man leaning against a tree handing out molded fruit cakes shaped like the svelte goddess. Livnath's priests chanting on their knees. Or the couple sipping from their soup bowls, moon amulets swinging from their necks. Each of them mingled among Aleph's pilgrims, unrepentant.

She and the Shamgar slowed their steps. The cliffs hung above them to the west. Legends said Aleph concealed remnants of his priests in the caves. But people couldn't always view the caves. Shammah didn't see them when he was with Peleg at Mount Aleph or during pilgrimages they took together.

Tamiym studied the pilgrims. Their open hunger to hear from the priests of the Existing One to emerge from the caves matched hers. She insisted she come on the pilgrimage alone, and she knew that offended Shammah, but he let her go. Her stomach moaned again. She drew out a dried fig from her pocket. She and Chazon were eating a bowl of freshly picked figs in the

Gardens of Destiny months ago when he had described Aleph's caves to her.

"The Existing One hid the priests during the days of Aikah and Kish," Chazon had said.

"Except for you," Tamiym said. "During the days of Aikah, with more priests alongside you, perhaps the king's rages would have stilled. You would have helped to woo more people to Aleph, and the Great War would never have happened."

Chazon smiled until his harsh brows softened. "Aikah, that king of blood, during his days of destruction, chose Shammah, who would one day succeed him. I spoke all that I could to him with the love I possessed. The love of a brother. Aleph gave Aikah the choice to listen. But it wasn't only Aikah in my care. The Existing One destined me to teach and protect Shammah. As Aleph led him to find you."

Tamiym paused on a grassy patch, palms on her heaving chest. Shammah also had found her. They met on the road to the City of Kings after the Four Faces guided him to Mount Aleph. Sadness struck her again as she remembered. A blow of longing followed. She was visiting the mountain without Shammah. Evading him in the palace had ushered in misery on the mountain.

The Shamgar stopped alongside her. Together, they waited for air to fill their lungs. When they started climbing again, a balding, bearded man with a runner's gait, clothed in a plain wool tunic, approached them. A priest of Aleph. Tamiym was certain of it. Fine, priestly robes embroidered with Livnath's name didn't drape his shoulders, neither did he appear breathless, hungry, ragged or unclean. The man loped toward them, completely at ease.

"Queen Tamiym." He bowed, but Tamiym wished she had bowed before him.

"You know me. Forgive me, but I do not know your name."

"Elihu. May I reassure you? Although enemies intrude these foothills, the servants of Aleph guard among the pilgrims."

"My lord, you ciphered my thoughts."

He bowed before the Shamgar standing close to her. "Unseen myriads keep watch with us."

"Can we see what you see?" Tamiym gazed at the cliffs and skies.

"A true pilgrim's desire." Elihu's unlined, copper-colored face shimmered in the starlight. "Questions pant within you. They form tiny peaks that rise skyward."

Thunder boomed. Tamiym and the Shamgar clustered together.

"Do not fear," Elihu said. "Sounds from the canopy of heaven. Aleph scatters light, covers the sea, and fills the earth."

"Do I search in vain, priest?"

"Who leads you on this search?"

"Who sets my soul aflame? Does Aleph plunder my soul or revive it? Darkness crushes my bones. I dream always of the dead. Does the Existing One seek my madness?"

"The Existing One broods over you. When you ascend the mountain, you will glimpse another facet of Aleph."

"Are you warning me?"

"Prepare."

Tamiym slid her knuckles across her face, feeling hot. "I do not know what that means."

"When you descend from the caves, do not return this way. Resist visiting your beloved queen mother in Yaphah as you planned. Keep going. Though the days smite you with pain, endure. Direction will be shown to you."

"From whom? A phantom bearing more despair?"

"A shopkeeper."

"Sir, do you wound intentionally? Am I a side of lamb for you to poke and pull? Must I troll the markets like the temple priestesses, my hand outstretched, seeking shopkeepers?"

"The shopkeeper will summon you."

"And how long will this be? My soul already shoulders the burden of eons. Release more sorrow upon my head after these twelve years of suffering, and my death will appear as happiness."

"Hardship will not slay you. Suffering will be a companion until the time for Aleph's swords."

The sky fell into full darkness, a dark, silken blue with a smattering of stars. The *kimah*. Elihu bowed. "Depart now."

His terse instructions didn't invite a farewell. Surely it was not his intent, but Elihu's promises made her feel cold and worn. Guriel climbed close beside her as they crossed a series of rocks. Sudden tears flowed as he gripped her arm. Such a slight, reassuring gesture from a seasoned bodyguard. Guriel didn't know it, but his presence uplifted her; for in the air, she sensed Shammah's comfort, reaching out to her in steadfast love.

One mourner lingered near the cemetery pit in Yaphah. Tears poured from Noadiah face, unconcerned that it had been hours since he stood there. A spattering of astrologers who called out to the stars as gods, and a few priests who read entrails, stood with him.

Noadiah didn't acknowledge them, the only son left to mourn her. He thought of her colorful textiles throughout their home, and how she murmured with a mysterious smile that Aleph gave her the power to sew. Newborns, elderly citizens, and the newly married of Yaphah often received quilts from her. The beauty of his mother's quilts helped him imagine the beauty of Aleph's throne. The hangers-on who haunted so many funerals in Yaphah cared only about money and influence; they didn't care about her generosity. Loneliness settled over him. How he wished his betrothed stood with him.

"My tributes are not enough for what you've done for me, Mother," he said.

He turned from the grave and walked among the tombs, wiping tears that continued to flow. His head was bowed when he heard a voice beside him.

"Son of Alita, do not mourn. You can see your mother again. Tonight."

The young man smelled old water, a polluted haven for insects and too slimy for cooking or bathing.

"Who are you? A friend of my mother's? I appreciate your presence, but the rites have ended."

The young man walked away. A hand, scaly and moist, pecked at his back.

"They have not. They have only begun."

Tamiym and the Shamgar reached a clearing. No longer did she smell broth and bread. Spices hung in the air. Na'iym, the only female Shamgar in the palace, the eighth in her family to serve as a bodyguard for the king, broke into a wide smile that Tamiym rarely saw.

Na'iym paused, tipping her face skyward. "Myrrh. Frankincense. Burnt *onycha* from the sea. *Galbanum.*"

"It's a gesture of love from the Existing One," said Amar, the third member of the Shamgar.

Ahead of them, small fires suddenly lit the caves. Tamiym breathed in short bursts. "How far do you think it is?"

"We can reach them in about an hour, my lady, if we hurry," Na'iym said.

Tamiym winced as pebbles rolled beneath the arches of her feet. The blister was worsening. She waved away Guriel and Amar when they tried to assist her. Being Shammah's queen had softened the artisan's daughter once accustomed to tending horses and cows and a small collection of crops.

Alongside her parents, Tamiym had fought to save young barley crops during a flood, saved goats from sandstorms whipping across their farm from the east, and hauled water from rare streams to the west. Living in the palace and growing older in limb, dulled the strength she boasted in Chaniya. *Almost.*

Just as the moon slid from behind the thick clouds, a woman with skin dark as raisins and swathed in a sapphire cloak blocked their path. The Shamgar circled Tamiym, swords drawn.

Guriel growled. "Of Aleph or Livnath?"

The woman never moved. "Queen Tamiym. We expected you."

The woman stood two shoulders above the Shamgar. Melodies and light leaped beside her. She extended a hand and immediately Tamiym and the Shamgar no longer stood on the mountainside. They sat shoeless and cross-legged in a cave by a small fire, ringed by seven hooded figures. Starlight stretching into the cave's opening and beamed inside.

Tamiym struggled to speak. "You know why I am here?"

One figure moved. He was a man. Lion-gold.

He leaned toward her. "We have sent you here."

Pain thrust Tamiym to Aleph. Not these strange creatures. "I do not understand," she said.

"A raging river always has a source. Did not circumstance drive you here?"

"I had no one else."

Thunder battered the quiet, and lightning, flaring from the east to the west, knifed through the sky. Tamiym and the Shamgar trembled.

"You knew who saw your need," the golden man said. "Aleph has not only seen it but answered."

"Death dragged my hopes into shadows years ago. Now dreams of death taunt me in the night watches."

The golden man outstretched his arms. "The word from Aleph is light."

In the semi-darkness, lush date palms and sparkling light sprang up between Tamiym and the Shamgar.

"The word from Aleph is a sword," the golden man said.

The Shamgar gasped as their weapons rattled. Amar opened his mouth to speak, but Na'iym placed a warning hand on his shoulder.

"The word from Aleph knows the heart of Aleph," the golden man said.

The six hooded ones who had said nothing leaned backward, hands to their chests. Tamiym felt a burning sensation and with it the fragrance that accompanied their climb. The scents encircled them, so tangible and comforting that Tamiym yearned to sleep.

The golden-haired man dropped his arms. "Aleph creates origins and endings. Nothing can compare with them, and nothing can defeat their purpose."

Sorrow had wrenched everything, and Tamiym couldn't lose this chance to make her plea. She shook off the longing for slumber. "Barrenness besets me. Only my dreams bring me peace. But I do not walk in rest. I spin between day truths and night visions. Is there no remedy?"

One of the hooded ones stood. Tamiym gasped when she realized it was the woman they met outside the cave.

"Great favor rests on you to serve Aleph, Queen Tamiym," the woman said. "Sadness haunts you now. New strength will come. Joy will follow."

"But I bear this alone."

"You have not. You do not. You will not."

The other five stood at once.

Tamiym scrambled to stand but couldn't. "Who are you?"

The golden man spoke first. "Insight."

Each of the others said their name.

"Wisdom."

"Understanding"

"Counsel."

"Power."

"Knowledge."

"Reverence for Aleph," concluded the woman in the sapphire cloak.

The man with the golden features concealed his features again. "Petition Aleph alone."

Tamiym and the Shamgar clasped hands, adjusting to the darkness. The figures waned before them like moonlight.

Once outside the cave, Tamiym and the Shamgar studied the fading pilgrim fires below.

Guriel drew his sword with a snap. "Elihu's words."

They nodded and searched for another way down the mountain.

*   *   *

Tamiym and the Shamgar reached the lower foothills as dawn dripped pink light on the rocky, treeless side of the mountain. Tamiym suspected the path they followed could be the one Shammah described from his first encounter on Mount Aleph years ago. The mountainside shifted, the Four Faces guided him, and the sapphire throne descended overhead.

Tamiym's right foot tapped a cluster of rocks, and she winced, bracing herself to howl. She stretched her right foot and untied her sandal to examine her heel.

Na'iym put out her torch and studied Tamiym's foot. "New skin replaced the blister, my lady," Na'iym said.

Tamiym nodded in gratitude. She retied her sandal with shaking hands. Aleph had healed her. As she bent over, a long piece of glittering scarlet cloth, about the length of an elephant's trunk, twirled between a knot of trees and shrubs, then rose on a breeze to a low-lying cliff where it clung to a rock, curling in the air.

The cloth could be hair ribbon. Or trim for a headdress. As she watched the cloth coil and uncoil, Tamiym relaxed. She breathed in the spices they had experienced earlier in the night and studied the ribbon, hoping that by standing still, the sensation of tenderness wouldn't leave.

A light breeze thrust the ribbon from its perch. The scent of spices fled. Tamiym rubbed her face, frustrated that she would have to wait before she could unlock the mystery of the spices and the scarlet cloth. Waiting and waiting had become as familiar as breathing.

A young girl, twirled a flower within a short distance of her parents, who prepared breakfast on a rocky portion of the mountain, surrounded by a few lambs. Shepherds. Not pilgrims. Tamiym stopped, curious.

"My lady, we must keep going," Guriel said.

"A moment," Tamiym said.

The girl was about seven or eight, petite and delicate. The smile on her face reminded Tamiym of how her baby daughter once curled her lips when she slept.

The girl outstretched her arms. "May I sing to you?"

"My lady, no," Guriel said.

Tamiym shrugged off Guriel's protective arm, the girl's pearly smile drawing her as the child sang:

Queen of none,
Shout the street children,
Ignorant and unclean,
Unknowing that a monarch to none is the destiny,
For the wisest know
That only the goddess chooses,
From sky to sun to moon to sea.

Tamiym gasped. Before she could pose a question, the girl's body dissolved into a crone — as haggard and beaten as the girl had been lovely and youthful.

"Who are you? What are you?" The words unwound within Tamiym's throat.

The crone lunged at Tamiym and the Shamgar. Tamiym pulled her sword from beneath her cloak and exchanged rounds with the crone as the Shamgar tried to overpower the crone from behind.

The crone turned, somersaulted above the soldiers, and held out her scrawny hand. From it spewed an inky darkness that tossed the Shamgar backward.

The crone returned her attention to Tamiym, responding to every jab Tamiym attempted. They dodged each other over the rocks. The crone cornered Tamiym and knocked away her sword. Tamiym lifted her head as the crone's sword dug into her chest, tearing into her heavy robe.

The crone paused before shoving her sword with the last nudge. "Your lies will haunt you in the underworld."

Tamiym clamped her eyes closed in prayer. *Insight. Wisdom. Understanding. Counsel. Power. Knowledge. Reverence for Aleph.* In a moment, light the hue of sapphires slit the space between Tamiym and the crone, who dropped her sword, howled, stung with pain. The crone reached for her sword but could not cross the light.

"Another time!"

The sapphire light, swirling like a dancing hand, chased the crone into a knot of trees.

The Shamgar joined Tamiym, dazed by the crone's assault. Guriel gulped for breath, bending to his knees.

"If you allow it, my lady, I will pursue the creature and drag her to your feet."

Two kings, decades of war, and age salted the gruff voice and deepened the lines from nose to jaw on Guriel. Wisdom outlasted the strong. Guriel would sacrifice anything, even himself, to protect the throne.

"No, faithful one," she said. "You warned me. I bear this. I ignored Elihu's words and placed the three of you in danger. Please forgive your queen. Pray my sorrow does not drive us into further recklessness."

Guriel pointed to the crone's sword. "What about this?"

"Leave it," Tamiym said. "Her weapons are not ours."

As Tamiym spoke, the sword crumpled into the rocks with a moan.

"The living weapon is gone," murmured Amar.

"Another work of Aleph," said Na'iym. She turned toward the clump of rocks where the crone had emerged. The fire disappeared, along with the couple. Only the crying lambs remained. "Aleph has driven them away."

Tamiym glanced further along the mountainside before exhaling in surprise.

Elihu.

The man raised his sapphire-studded staff, and the lambs scurried toward him obediently as the sun soared into full day.

Gila and Eitan dismounted and walked alongside their horses. The stars hung low. Gila wanted to reach and clasp them. Watching the stars bloom every night soothed her, as had her marriage to the commander. Eitan, wells of unexpected rivers and mountain streams for her parched heart, watered her days with contentment. Despite this, Gila didn't feel secure. Minacious ones she couldn't identify creeped near them.

"What fills your mind, Gila," Eitan said.

"Restlessness."

"In war, you feel it. You reach for shield and spear without thought because you sense the enemy before you feel his breath."

"I should call it dread."

"This is about Shammah and Tamiym."

"My heart aches for them."

They stopped and Mount Aleph loomed in view, shadowed beneath the sky threaded with stars and clouds. Gila allowed herself to feel the breeze lift the hairs on her arm and graze her tunic. She was happy to move to Yaphah and away from the City of Kings. Pageantry and the ease of the palace paled compared to these evenings with Eitan beneath skies that displayed riches greater than the king's treasuries. However, the distance from Shammah and Tamiym left Gila vulnerable to worries she couldn't dispel.

"I have also seen things I cannot explain."

Eitan took the reins from her and released their horses to roam in the grasses before winding an arm around her shoulders. "Sweet one. What have you seen that disturbs you?"

"An apparition appeared near the tombs. At first, I feared it was a foul rumor. The wives who I spend time with making clothes told me this. Then I saw one of them, hugging the wall like a shadow near our home."

"Why did you not warn me? Were your bodyguards with you?"

She moved closer to him. "I saw the shadow from the balcony. My love, I fear they are princes from the dark realms of the Time Sea."

"Yaphah may be the origin site for war. We always suspected Dahv and his conspirators fled to the Water People, and that Mahalath joined them. But for more than a decade, they have done nothing."

Gila shuddered. "They were waiting."

The river ran blue, white, and fast. Finding a patch to sit on and wiggle his toes proved more difficult than Naphtali expected. He should have kept on his sandals. The moist grass cleansed the dust on his feet, but his slow pace didn't promise that he would escape sharp rocks hidden by clumps of grass and reeds.

The river kept its promise, though. The thrust of water pushing over the rocks in rhythm, gladdened like a hymn. Lady Abigail sang hymns when she thought no one was listening. Sometimes Naphtali wondered if she knew he listened, curled on the stairs while she cooked.

He displeased her this afternoon. Only a few days ago, she returned from the City of Kings with barely a chirp after visiting with Iyar. During the visit, Lady Abigail met Raushanna, the mysterious woman who drove Iyar to overeat dates when she refused to see him and ignited unexpected kindnesses when they sang together.

Naphtali couldn't be certain, but as Abigail marshaled everyone from the household to the scribal school, she seemed pensive after meeting Raushanna. She asked him questions about the musician before falling into a weighty silence that deepened Naphtali's personal gloom. This was his twenty-second year. For twelve years, he clung to Abigail's words that Aleph would speak to him. He had heard nothing. No visions appeared to him.

For months, his frustrations increased. Naphtali felt like an apple being cored by a heavy hand. Today started badly.

Every instruction Lady Abigail gave, he partially followed. He dropped two fresh tablets. He mercilessly quizzed several pupils on their handling of their styluses.

Lady Abigail placed her hands on his shoulders. "If the pupils hear any more of you, they may run home to their mothers, Naphtali. Return when what ails you flees."

Ailing him was the monotony of waiting, and with it, his yearning to change from adolescent to man. Naphtali longed for his circumstances to match the heavy volume in his voice and the scratchy hairs of his beard. Naphtali saw less of Abigail when he wanted to speak with her most. He had questions for her, but she focused either on the school or Chazon when he was home.

Abigail said Aleph was going to call him. Naphtali didn't know if the Existing One would stand amid Abigail's orchards and call out to him or shout while he slept. It was too confusing. What made sense were the genealogy tablets from Iyar and Abigail's ancestors. For twelve years, and in secrecy, the pupils in Abigail's school had made multiple copies for six gates. Only work for the tablet designated for the Seventh Gate required completion.

Naphtali often mused about whether he should rejoin Iyar's caravans. He hadn't forgotten the pirates they fought, the bargains they discovered, the deserts they crossed. While he didn't miss Iyar's cart load of curses and cruelties, the merchant had softened. When Naphtali visited, he acknowledged the boy in his curt way. A wound was still there, but his kinder nature? Naphtali credited the pragmatic and generous Hulda. Naphtali grunted. He also credited himself. Naphtali no longer was a boy.

A circular mound of grass invited, and Naphtali plopped there and dropped a toe into the lapping water near it. When would Aleph call his name? He dreamed often of the founding. The stories the two tablets told became companions. He knew the families, how they settled, how they multiplied, and how they started a new life, the dread of another deluge sweeping away family members never escaping their thoughts.

The elders selected Iyar and Abigail's family as leaders because of their faithfulness, which made Naphtali jealous to know his own family. He wished he and Hulda could trace their lineage to the first generations after the Deluge. They could go no further than his parents pledging to marry in the Cove of Revealing, where neither he nor Hulda could even remember because they were babes.

Their parents moved to the City of Kings because King Aikah needed ship makers, a trade his father excelled in. Naphtali could remember those family times together when his parents prospered. They had a two-story house and his mother cooked for several families. He started school and Hulda worked with his mother. Then the Great War seized their happiness.

Hulda didn't enjoy talking much about the past, and Naphtali suspected she rolled it away like kneading bread and piled it somewhere where he couldn't see. She was the eldest and always behaved like that. Concealing thoughts. Protecting him. Perhaps he would benefit from more stoicism, for his heart throbbed in pain or pleasure, causing weeping or shouting when he least wanted to. Lady Abigail was right; leaving the school for a while settled his thoughts.

Water lapping on his toes also helped. He dug his feet deeper in the water, watching it pool around his ankles. He stood, looking for something to grip. He found more rocks and curled his toes around them to stand. The water was warm.

Then too warm. He tried to pull out his feet, but something twirled around his right ankle. He bent toward the clear water. A serpent. Naphtali wriggled his ankle, but the serpent grasped harder. Naphtali could feel its heat grow.

Standing awkwardly with his feet planted on the riverbank, Naphtali found two rocks. One for the tail. One for the head. If he could see them both, he could crush the serpent on both ends and disentangle his ankle.

The water bubbled as the snake arched its back to strike. Its tail twisted as it wrapped around Naphtali's leg. Naphtali slammed a rock against the tail, crying out because he also struck his calf. The serpent jerked and, in one movement, Naphtali drove the serpent's head into the mud of the river. Blood from the snake seeped green.

Naphtali jumped from the water. Gasping as he ran his fingers over his legs. No wounds. But there would be a mighty bruise.

He stumbled away from the river to a tree. He hadn't seen a serpent. Since… He could not pinpoint a time. And he didn't know why he killed it the way he did, disabling the creature and saving his life.

He gaped at the river, which still raced past him. The water rippled near the rocks where Naphtali stood moments ago. Rising from the waters was a giant, screeching serpent. Its teeth appeared jutted like many knives, and the creature bore green eyes and a colossal head. No, two. No… Naphtali kept watching. Seven heads. *The beast had seven heads.* They bobbed in the waters surging around them.

Naphtali felt the rough bark as he pressed against the tree. This was another vision. He hadn't seen a vision since the wedding of Queen Tamiym and King Shammah. Why now?

The serpent tossed the waters with a violence that dispersed the birds. River reeds curled in dread. Grasses drooped. Behind him, the tree groaned, and its bark crackled. Naphtali hopped up, ready to flee. The serpent emerged from the water, its scales and heads folded behind him. A man pale as bread dough, in a bedraggled tunic, covered in seaweed, stood on the shore.

You will one day fight him.

Naphtali spun around on one foot. Where did those words come from? He looked back at the serpent-man. The man's mouth never moved.

"I spoke to you, Naphtali. I have called you."

Aleph.

The voice was deep, like drums flanked with notes from a lyre. Chazon told him once that the voice of Aleph surprises. Aleph had spoken to him on a muddy riverbank as a serpent-man threatened him.

"Aleph?" Naphtali fell to his knees. "What do you want from me?"

"To become the warrior who fights this dragon."

"Me?" Naphtali asked. He gawked at the serpent-man, who slowly backed into the water, the dragon shell covering him again as he slid into the water.

"Seth will need your sword."

"I must rely on you, Existing One. To wield a weapon." Naphtali felt his heart pounding and his stuttering increasing. "My sword lessons are lacking. My training is insufficient. Chazon says that when we practice. I disappoint him. I certainly disappointed Lord Iyar. But I was only a boy then. Boys aren't reliable with swords, are they?"

"You do not disappoint me, Naphtali. Rely on me. Even when your sword work falters. Only my measures matter and not the weights of men who see visions and speak prophecies only in part."

Naphtali crunched his forehead in a frown. "Is that why you had me wait? To teach me that? I have seen no recent visions until today. I never heard your voice until today. I thought you would never call me. Now it is my anxiety that seems futile. Was that the lesson?"

Honeyed laughter boomed around the youth as Naphtali gawked in wonder. Naphtali couldn't see who was speaking, but Aleph's laughter commissioned and commanded.

The dragon figure fully disappeared, the birds returned with a song, the grasses and reeds raised upright like dancers, and the tree no longer moaned. Butterflies bounced near Naphtali, skipping from grasses to roses. A small, golden butterfly landed on his shoulder.

"Your laughter changes everything." Naphtali stared at the butterfly.

"Joy defeats calamity," Aleph said. "Rely on me for joy. It will be your sword."

"First, may I honor you. As I would a mortal king." Naphtali bowed deeply as the butterfly sprang away. "I submit to you, Lord Aleph. I pledge allegiance to a magnificence that summons the earth. Its creatures bow to your voice."

"Your soul sees where your eyes cannot."

The laughter from Aleph became a cheerful hum, the sounds made by a pleased man after feasting on roasted lamb. Naphtali smiled at the contented sound, bobbing his head on his shoulder, searching for someone he could see. Or touch.

Questions jostled in his mind like children vying for attention at their father's knee.

Naphtali kicked the grass with his bare feet, locks of hair sliding on his forehead. "You mentioned a sword. Don't I need a sword in my hand?"

"I gave you two rocks to kill the river serpent. Is it impossible for me to supply a sword?"

"My Lord Aleph, was that you? And was it you who filled my mind on how to conquer it? You saved my life from poison. I'll have a bruise, though. Lady Abigail will think I fell. Or followed some mischief."

More laughter. This time, the sound wrapped around Naphtali like the wind.

"Return to the river."

Naphtali hesitated. The river-serpent nearly bit him and the vision of the seven-headed serpent enclosing a man triggered fears he didn't know he possessed. Naphtali bit his lip. He didn't want to disappoint Aleph — especially since they were getting acquainted.

Heat flooded Naphtali's face. Why was he a soldier without arrows or spear? Always the fearful boy, never prepared for war? Aleph's hum became a murmur. A rocking sound, a lullaby for the discomfited. "Remember what happened when I laughed? From my laughter, draw strength."

Naphtali tiptoed to the riverbank, his foot shaking, his hands clenched, waiting for a hiss in the grass. He should have picked up rocks to carry. Another snake could come hunting for his flesh.

At the river's edge, he saw multi-colored pebbles. Those weren't here before. No sign of the green blood was there, either. Naphtali kept looking. Slightly covered by water, lay a jeweled sword on the brilliant pebbles.

Naphtali lifted the sword from the cold water. When he closed his hand over the sword, it felt like a second hand. He lifted it skyward. A finger like a man's whirled around the blade and scrawled blood-red words into the weapon.

"What do you see written, Naphtali?" Laughter still leaped in Aleph's voice.

"Sea of Joy."

When Naphtali reached Abigail's door, he suddenly didn't know what to say. He stayed at the house closer to the scribal school, not this one that Lady Abigail and the priest Chazon shared since their marriage.

Roses bloomed near the large windows. The topaz-colored house often invited him to lean against its walls to read a tablet or sleep, which he often did when he finished his chores.

None of those urges wrestled with him today. Aleph had spoken to him, given him the sword that was tied to his waist, and summoned him to a war.

Naphtali pulled the sword out again. Sea of Joy. With this sword, he was going to defeat a seven-headed serpent-dragon someday. He turned. Abigail probably was still at the scribal school. He didn't know why he had stopped here first.

The door swung opened. It was Chazon, hair popping from his head like weeds, his rough tunic askew. "Why are you standing at the door? What do you want?"

Chazon rubbed his face and peered at the sword. "Where did you get that?"

The priest reached for it, but Naphtali stepped back. "It's the sword of Aleph. He gave it to me. By the river. And I saw a serpent with seven heads. But it looked like a man, too. A man that needed scrubbing. Seaweed covered him."

Chazon gasped as if he had been running. "Wait. Stay right here," he said.

The priest returned, tidy, with a low rumble in his voice. "We must find Abigail."

They raced through the date orchard to the scribal school and saw Abigail dismissing the children to their homes. Some pupils tried to straggle, like the brother and sister who ogled Naphtali when he taught them their lessons. But the pair scrambled to the door as Abigail shooed the students outside.

Deborah, a girl about Naphtali's age and height, slowly picked up her tablets, then glided past him with a smile. Naphtali blushed when her elbow brushed his.

"We missed you during our tablet study, Naphtali." Deborah smiled again.

Naphtali gulped. Rosebuds paled compared with Deborah's lips. She deserved a hymn dedicated to her, but all he could do was stare, smitten.

Abigail waved Deborah toward the threshold. "Go, child. Lessons resume tomorrow."

After closing the door, Abigail rained clipped glances on Naphtali and Chazon. "You two look as agitated as camels who want to lounge and not travel. Chazon, I left you sleeping. Why have you left your bed? Naphtali, I told you to rest. Your irritation spilled over to the pupils. Why did you both ignore my instructions?"

Chazon marched around them, hands behind his back. "He received the call, Abigail."

Abigail's sternness dissipated when she fell to a bench. "The ways of Aleph. An ordinary day from sunup to sundown. Within it, a gust of revelation. Naphtali, tell us what happened. Please."

"I heard Aleph. He showed me how to kill a serpent in the nearby river. With two stones. A dragon with seven heads appeared. Inside it was a man, filthy and aged. Aleph interrupted the vision. He said I will fight this man-serpent one day. The man returned to the water as a dragon. And Aleph laughed. He laughed like a man. Not a small laugh. A loud laugh like the noisy sounds you hear in the taverns when the plump men drink too much."

Abigail and Chazon both exchanged glances. Naphtali sighed. "What I mean to say is that it was a roaring laugh. Also, a commanding laugh," Naphtali said. "The grass, the flowers, the water, the trees, and the butterflies danced to his laughter. Oh. Aleph hummed. Not like Livnath in the tablets. Remember how the goddess hummed dangerously to Iyar and Zetham? When Aleph hums, it isn't like that. Afterward, Aleph gave me this."

Naphtali handed the sword to Abigail.

Chazon grunted. "Why do you let Lady Abigail touch it and I cannot?"

"She serves as the midwife of this moment," Naphtali said.

Abigail held the sword and skillfully twirled it with her hands before pointing it toward Naphtali's chin. "You pledged allegiance, did you not?"

Naphtali struggled to concentrate as Abigail held the sword before him. Could joy and death greet him in a single day?

"I could do nothing else. I never saw Aleph. His presence encircled me with laughter. The sound of mirth wooed me to pledge myself to him. Earth responds to his voice. How could I resist?"

"Have you told him what this day means?" Chazon asked Abigail.

She gently handed the sword back to Naphtali, noting the engraving, *Sea of Joy*. "Naphtali, you are now the seventh scribe. I could not allow you to work on the third tablet until you pledged allegiance to Aleph. For that to happen, the Existing One had to call you first."

"Why didn't he call me long ago? I was ready when you brought me to Nifla."

"I think not, Naphtali. Every day you waited for your life to change, and yet, every day, you served. You had no choice."

"Aleph disciplined you. Like a son," Chazon said. "Today he rewarded you. Like a son.

"By giving you the sword, Aleph summoned you to serve him in battle. War and deliverance can begin."

"Why war? I am no one. Isn't it enough that I must face a dragon? What if there are more dragons?"

"Sit," Chazon said. "Remember when I first met you all those years ago?"

"Yes," Naphtali said, adjusting his sword awkwardly before he found a stool. "I was a gnat in your sight. Lady Abigail corrected you. Is she the only person you heed, Lord Chazon?"

"That is uncalled for," Chazon began.

After Abigail elbowed him, the priest readjusted in mid-sentence. *Chazon should thank Aleph that Abigail didn't deliver a greater punishment*, Naphtali thought. She could have forced the priest to sweep the floors. Naphtali once swept them all night when he refused to listen to Abigail's warning to be quiet.

Naphtali nodded his head with approval until Chazon bowed before him.

"To my shame, I spoke before seeing," Chazon continued. "I seek your forgiveness again. Never follow in my steps with that error. It would be foolhardy. What Lady Abigail encouraged me to *see* was what Aleph intended us to *know*. You descend from a great tribe. Your family dates to those decades after the Great Deluge. To the founding of Seth. Your ancestor knew the first Iyar and his sons."

"My family associated with the first Iyar? By the pigs and rats." Naphtali caught himself. "Accept my repentance, Lady Abigail. How odd is that? My ancestors were friends with the first Iyar and his descendant didn't want to pay me a shekel."

"Ah. But his sister did," Chazon said. "And she brought you to her home. And gave you employment."

Naphtali blushed. "For which I am grateful. But I read the first two tablets since I've been here. May it not be that my family was one of those horrid elders. They threw the first Iyar over the cliff as his wife pleaded for her husband to live."

"Your father's ancestor was the first Patal. He was traveling when the tragedy occurred and regretted being unable to defend Iyar and his family. Once Livnath seized Ariel, and with no evidence of Aleph's tablets to show Aleph's claim, your ancestor settled in the Cove of Everlasting. Until his death, he petitioned Aleph that one day he or his descendants would fight to ensure Aleph's rightful ownership of Seth and Ariel, which we know as the City of Kings. Generations have passed with his hopes waiting on the clouds, but Aleph chose you to answer your ancestor's petitions."

Naphtali fell quiet. He had never connected his family to what he read in the first two tablets. He would have to see Hulda soon. Or send a messenger. They could wonder together what kind of man their ancestor was. Was he tall like their father? Was he from a fishing family like their parents, and could he serenade the dolphins in the Cove of Everlasting?

Abigail interrupted Naphtali's musings. "Such knowledge can overwhelm anyone, Naphtali."

"I cannot grasp what Aleph has done. But only this is my question. Do you know if my ancestor stumbled over his words? Like I do?"

"It does not matter, Naphtali," Chazon said. "You fulfill your ancestor's earnest petitions. You are dew in the morning, a gift longed for."

Naphtali looked away. Embarrassed. Tears reddened Chazon's eyes.

Abigail opened a cabinet and pulled out the original three tablets. The glowing desert colors of the four horsemen draped them.

"The fabric is intact." Naphtali became ridiculously happy.

"Pulling from the skills of our father, Yissack, Iyar repaired the torn fabric," Abigail said, her face beaming.

"It took him years," Chazon said. "Gabar painstakingly showed Iyar where to retrieve the ingredients to create the hues."

"He also provided a covering," Abigail said. She pulled a heavy cloth from the cabinet. Sewn into the cloth was the name, "Patal."

Naphtali rubbed his fingers over the cloth.

"Iyar offers this to you as a friend. Not as a master."

Naphtali touched the fabric. His shoulders trembled. Based on the intricate design, Naphtali knew it was his former master's because it bore Iyar's stylish olive leaves. He sighed. Iyar was asking for forgiveness and offering peace.

"Patal authored the third tablet," Abigail continued. "As you will learn soon, Patal wrestled to write it. And, along with those of us who follow Aleph, you will wrestle to protect them all."

Iyar waved off a slave who accompanied him. *Let the man go home*. No one would attack him in the streets. Not where he intended to go. And especially since the thick clouds promised a downpour.

The night walks had become Iyar's habit for months. Hulda started preparing bread for him to carry as he meditated along the narrow streets of the City of Kings. Every night, when Iyar visited Livnath's temple site, he trudged like a man veiled by stealth, a man burdened by secrets. After each visit, he noticed that the heavy rains chewed away at the temple foundation and the tower's first platform. The unfinished temple stood in shadow before Iyar. He stopped, then bellowed: "Why?"

Iyar didn't expect an answer the dozens of times he stopped at this same point on the temple grounds. He didn't expect one tonight. He kept walking until he heard horses stomping.

He turned in all directions. No carts wobbled on the street, so he dismissed the thought and resumed his stroll. He flexed his arms. He always felt better after the walks because they helped him sleep.

Iyar was yawning when he glimpsed light at the temple steps. Iyar stopped. No one worked at night. Oil was too valuable. Iyar looked closer. Chaggay, his head hung low, squatted in the mud beside an oil lamp. Iyar sloughed a path toward the merchant. "Why are you here? Are you unwell?"

Chaggay, who sat at the temple's second platform, gave Iyar the faraway stare of the drugged. Poppy pots and strange brews often lined Chaggay's elaborate feasting tables when he hosted the nobles. Sips of poppy juice may have addled Chaggay's thoughts and led him to the ruins.

"Are you here to witness my demise, Iyar? To cackle over my downfall?"

"Your downfall? Let me help you home."

"My downfall, my ruin. First, it was drought. It slowed the construction by years. Do not pretend you did not know. Then it was the downpours. Because of the extended rains, my shekels are disappearing faster than I can replace them. I cannot buy the materials I need to maintain the mud-brick houses I built, and I cannot underwrite my part of the contract. Ezer has threatened to pull me from the contract. I will lose all the money I poured into the temple. The priests will own everything."

"Do you have financial reserves in barley, tin or copper?"

"Gone. The priests also accuse me of cheating and adding other metals to my silver shekels."

"Did you?"

"I was desperate." Chaggay moaned. "My wife threatened to leave me when the first mud-brick homes fell. Remember that scandal? Three years ago. King Shammah brought in stone, but I was too proud to ask for more help. I thought the rains would cease their fierce onslaught. They did, for a while. Not anymore. Weeks of rain have badly damaged the foundation. The drains continue to clog. The stone the priests imported is not enough to save the temple structure. Or me."

Clouds swelled. Rain drops fell. When Iyar gazed west of the temple, Iyar saw Gabar and the horsemen with their black steeds. He gulped. He *had* heard horses. Multi-colored light obscured the horsemen's faces. But the steeds, through their ferocious, untamed eyes, shouted: *It is time.*

"Chaggay," Iyar said. "May I make you an offer?"

"A bargain with me? I have nothing to negotiate. Perhaps you merely want to gloat?"

"I want to pay off your debts. Reestablish your business."

"What will you require in return?"

"First, your trust. After that, your contract with the priests. And after that, your testimony before the king."

"But you do not serve Livnath."

"And I never will. The plans I spoke about twelve years ago to the council-court remain. I want to build a series of gardens that can help feed and increase prosperity to the City of Kings."

"You are sincere? You pledge to restore my provision?"

"With might greater than mine, I promise to settle every debt."

"Then the contract is yours. Our scribes will meet in the morning, and I agree to testify before the king."

Iyar outstretched his hand. Chaggay hesitated before grabbing it and standing. The clouds heaved dark and gray. Rain rushed over both men. Drenching their tunics. They guffawed like youths whose voices had suddenly deepened.

"Hulda will fuss about my soiled clothes. She will complain to Keziah. They will not spare me."

"My heart has stopped pounding. Iyar, I could embrace you for a hundred moons."

"Please, do not. You are wet. Muddy. And smelly."

Chaggay chortled without offense. "Then may I sing a hymn at my feasting table? I will hire the best musicians."

Iyar laughed as they sloshed through the mud. Tears streamed down Iyar's cheeks because he heard melodies soaring above them. "Ah," Iyar said. "Why not sing together?"

If you enjoyed The Lost Tablets of Iyar,
please post a review.

**Some dragon stories are too real
to be untrue.**

THE SHIELDS
OF THE EARTH

SEVEN GATES OF THE
KINGDOM BOOK 3

Coming October 2022

In the meantime, to show my appreciation for all the
loyal readers of this series, please visit the link below for a
***FREE* short story** that connects *The Lost Tablets of Iyar*
to the next book, *The Shields of the Earth*.

GREEN MIST AND FIRE

A Seven Gates of the Kingdom Short Story

Download your free copy with this link:
https://BookHip.com/FMDPHKA

ABOUT THE AUTHOR

A former newspaper journalist, J. H. Ellis enjoys chai, a fresh cup of masala and walks with her husband Oscar and their Jack-Chi Shakespeare. You can chat with J.H. Ellis on Instagram or on Twitter at jhellismusingsandbooks and @JudyHowardEllis.

SEVEN GATES OF THE KINGDOM SERIES

The Gate of Aleph (Seven Gates of the Kingdom Book 1)

The Amber Whirlwind (Seven Gates of the Kingdom Book 1.5)

The Lost Tablets of Iyar (Seven Gates of the Kingdom Book 2)
– September 2022

Green Mist and Fire (Seven Gates of the Kingdom Book 2.5)

The Shields of the Earth (Seven Gates of the Kingdom Book 3)
– October 2022